Me and Sophie had this song. Well, it was her song but I kind of adopted it too. She'd found it on iTunes or some other download site. An old tune from the 1980s that her mum told her about. The band was called Yargo and the song was all about trying to get to your lover, who was far away. Sophie loved that song. It took a while but it grew on me too and we used to make references to it all the time because it was like our thing. And then she went off and all I ___ ___ ___ that tune. And only in my head bec___ ___ ___ ___ my music library when she ___ ___ ___ ___ ___ aybe. I dunno.

It's called 'Get The ___ ___ ___ ___ d it's swimmin' round in my he___ ___ ___ go away. I sometimes dream up ways of g___ ___ the memory. Like can I cut a hole in my head and get some tweezers and pull it out? Like the way Sophie pulled out my eyebrow hairs when we were in Year 11, pinning me down on her bed and giggling. Calling me a tranny. But I can't forget that song. It won't go away. We made a promise to each other – to always be friends, no matter what happened. I told her that even if she disappeared from the face of the earth, I'd find her. I'd get to her. I just never thought that it would happen.

Critical acclaim for *The Last Taboo*:
'A powerful depiction of family history, cultural prejudice and gang culture . . . hard-hitting' *The Bookseller*

And for *Rani & Sukh*:
'This powerful read is unforgettable, 5 stars out of 5' *Mizz*
'Overwhelmingly powerful' *The Bookseller*

And for *(un)arranged marriage*:
'Absorbing' *Observer*

Also by Bali Rai:

(un)arranged marriage
the crew
Rani & Sukh
The Whisper
The Last Taboo

www.balirai.co.uk

BALI RAI

the
angel collector

Corgi Books

THE ANGEL COLLECTOR
A CORGI BOOK 978 0 552 55302 5

Published in Great Britain by Corgi Books,
an imprint of Random House Children's Books

This edition published 2007

1 3 5 7 9 10 8 6 4 2

Set in 12/14pt Bembo Schoolbook by
Falcon Oast Graphic Art Ltd.

Corgi Books are published by Random House Children's Books,
61–63 Uxbridge Road, London W5 5SA

www.**kids**at**randomhouse**.co.uk

Addresses for companies within The Random House Group Limited can be found at:
www.randomhouse.co.uk/offices.htm

THE RANDOM HOUSE GROUP Limited Reg. No. 954009

A CIP catalogue record for this book is available from the British Library.

Printed in the UK by CPI Bookmarque, Croydon, CR0 4TD

For Jag, my beautiful Geordie girl, with all my love. Thank you for being there for me. Even when I'm a mardy git . . . And for Simran too. x x x

And for the usual suspects: Penny and Jennifer; Lucy, Annie and all at RHCB.

The rusty padlock hit the ground with a soft thud as the howling wind blew dirt into his eyes. Reflexes closed his eyelids – but too late. Little particles of grit lodged themselves against his corneas, scratching and stinging. He swore out loud and steadied himself, rubbing his eyes. It took a few moments for him to open them again, and when he did they were watering and sore. He swore again.

The cover flap for the lock fell back and he pulled the creaking door open, just enough for him to squeeze through the gap. The vicious smell from inside the out-building burned his nostrils as he flicked his torch on. Shining it towards the back wall, he saw her trying to move but restrained by the tape that tied her to the chair. Tied her to him . . .

He edged inside and drew the door shut behind him, bolting it from the inside. The torch threw a long, narrow beam of light and he followed it, towards her. As he approached she wriggled some more, aware of him. He stood for a moment and watched her and he felt thrilled, excited. Ashamed of himself, he set the portable cassette player he was holding down on the filthy floor, biting his bottom lip to stifle the scream he knew was coming. As he let it pass silently his whole body shook and his eyes tried to turn themselves inside out. He shuddered and let his bottom lip go. Crouching, he turned on the cassette player; music filled cold spaces with warmth. The cold space he was standing in and the cold space in his soul . . .

He walked slowly over to her and knelt in front of the chair, his knees sliding in the human detritus that a body has to cast off. The smell that rose from the floor made him fight back dry heaves and he had to turn his head as the particles in his eyes began to bite again. He closed his eyes and let the music fill his mind and take the bad things away. It took a minute or so, but soon he was calm again; he turned back to her, lifted his hands to her face and pushed the blindfold up onto her forehead. Bright blue eyes looked back at him, full of emotion, sending his mind into a spin. This angel really did love him. She was ready to take her place . . .

When it was over he walked slowly across to the door and stopped for a second to turn back and look at her in the narrow shaft of light. He felt the anger and pain rise in his throat and this time he let himself scream, a deep, guttural sound that let out everything he held inside. He turned and opened the door, wiping his mouth with his forearm. Then he wiped his forearm against his jeans, shuddering when he saw the mixture of saliva and blood that snaked a trail down his leg . . .

One

'You'll find someone else.'

It was one of the last things that Sophie said to me in person. Face to face rather than sent in a text or email. The last time I saw her face before she went off with her friends. She couldn't look at me, didn't see the way I was trying to fight back tears, like a child. Maybe she didn't want to see how much of a knob I was, getting all upset and that. Dunno. She didn't look though. Just carried on speaking.

'Some really cute girl when you're out one night—'

'No.'

'You will – an' we'll get back to the way it was before . . . like family. Before all this complicated stuff started—'

'Is that what I am now?' I spat out, not meaning to sound angry.

'Jit . . .'

This time she did look, right into my eyes. I got all embarrassed, wiped my eyes, looked away. She put her hand on mine. I pulled my hand away.

'I'm *sorry*,' she insisted, but sorry didn't do me no

good. It didn't make things right in my head. And I told her.

'Jit . . . I can't do this if you're gonna be—'

'What?' I shouted. 'A wanker?'

'Don't swear at me,' she warned.

'I'm not swearin' at you,' I replied. 'I'm just . . .'

'Upset. And angry and pissed off – and I'm really sorry but what do you want me to tell you? That I love you like *that* when I don't . . . I can't . . .?'

I stood up, wiped my eyes and looked at her. 'I can't be arsed with this any more,' I told her.

'But we have to sort it out, Jit – before I go—'

'Send me a text,' I said as the waitress who'd brought us our coffees gave me a funny look, like she knew I was being brushed off. Like she felt sorry for me. This thing in my brain started to pound and I glared at her.

'You wanna autograph?' I asked her, instantly feeling like a dickhead.

'*Jit!*' I heard Sophie shout as I ran out of the door and into the crowds in Leicester city centre.

Me and Sophie had this song. Well, it was her song but I kind of adopted it too. She'd found it on iTunes or some other download site. An old tune from the 1980s that her mum told her about. The band was called Yargo and the song was all about trying to get to your lover, who was far away. Sophie loved that song. It took a while but it grew on me too and we used to make references to it all the time because it was like our thing. And then she went off and all I had left was that tune. And only in my head because I'd deleted it from my music library when she went. Like an act of revenge maybe. I dunno.

It's called 'Get There' – the song. Sophie's song. And it's swimmin' round in my head right now. Won't go away. I sometimes dream up ways of getting rid of the memory. Like can I cut a hole in my head and get some tweezers and pull it out? Like the way Sophie pulled out my eyebrow hairs when we were in Year 11, pinning me down on her bed and giggling. Calling me a tranny. But I can't forget that song. It won't go away. We made a promise to each other – to always be friends, no matter what happened. I told her that even if she disappeared from the face of the earth, I'd find her. I'd get to her. I just never thought that it would happen.

Year 9

Sophie's note, dated 21 October:

Hey Jit –
fancy a snog???????
X ♡ X ♡ X ♡ X ♡ X ♡ X ♡ X

Sophie's email, dated 23 October:

The least you could do is reply, young man. It took me ages to pluck up the courage to write that note. I had to have a stiff brandy to get the nerve and you don't even reply. What's the matter – are you shy? I was only kidding about the snog anyway. I thought we could be friends though – lol!!! I even told my dad about you – he smiled. By the way, in case you were wondering, I got your email address from Sharon Culverwell in 9TM. She really fancies you. Can't see why though. Your legs are too skinny. Check out the link below for a really funny joke . . .

Two

Sophie's mum, Imogen, answered the door. Her hair had turned grey overnight; back in the previous July, when she first found out that Sophie had vanished. It was eight months on from that night and now her hair was lank and greasy and clumps of it had fallen out.

'Jit? Let me put my hat on,' she said, looking embarrassed.

I stood where I was in the rain, waiting to be asked in.

'What are you doing?' asked Imogen, adjusting the black cap.

'Er . . . you didn't say to come in, Mrs Davis.'

She gave me a funny look. 'Since when did that matter? And why are you calling me Mrs Davis?'

The truth was I wasn't sure whether I was doing the right thing. So I didn't feel ready to step over the threshold and tell her what was on my mind. She was going to do one of two things. Tell me that I was crazy and to get out. Or tell me to call the police. And I wasn't about to waste my time with the second one.

Not after eight months of nothing but empty promises and failed investigations.

'Well . . . ?' she asked, looking impatient.

I stepped into the hallway, let her close the heavy wooden door and followed her into the huge kitchen. She sat down at the round table and I stood leaning against a run of cupboards, just like I always did.

'I was marking a load of essays,' she told me.

'I'm sorry – I can come back another time . . .'

Sophie's mum smiled at me. It was a genuine smile but it was tired and worn and broken too. 'Sit down, you daft sod . . .'

I walked over to the table and took a chair, looking down at a copy of the *Independent* that was open at page seven. There was a story about a missing teenager called Kylie Simmons and someone had ringed parts of the text in black ink.

'Stephen did that,' Imogen said quietly.

'What?'

She nodded at the story about the missing girl.

'Oh . . .' I replied, my thoughts immediately turning to Sophie. I wondered if that's what had made her dad, Stephen, notice the story about Kylie Simmons. It must have done, I told myself.

'He's upstairs,' continued Imogen.

I nodded, looking around the room. The light coming in through the window was tinged with pink. Outside the clouds had darkened and the plants appeared to glow. Something seemed to be leeching the light from the sky. I looked across the table to an alcove that was inset with three thick wooden shelves. The middle one had a few photo frames on it and my gaze stuck on the one furthest to the left. It showed Sophie, with her mum and dad. They were standing in front of a marine centre in Florida, drenched in water and suntans, laughing and holding each other. In the next frame along was a picture of Sophie arm in arm with her best friend, Jenna, taken in a city centre bar. To the left of the picture was a hand holding a fag and a San Miguel. It was my left hand.

'Have you seen much of Jenna?' I asked, not knowing what else to say and prompted by the photo.

Imogen nodded. 'She was round here the other day – said that she'd seen you at some club. With a girl . . .'

I looked at her and felt a tear well up. I looked away quickly.

'So . . . who's the lucky lady?' asked Imogen, doing her best to sound happy.

'No one,' I said. 'Just a girl, that's all . . .'

She gave me another strange look and then asked me if I'd eaten. I shook my head, hoping that she wouldn't lecture me. Knowing that she would.

'But you need to eat properly,' she told me. 'You're in Year Twelve now – all that hard work uses up energy.'

'It *would* be hard if I found it difficult,' I told her.

'It can't *all* be easy, surely,' she said, getting up and checking on a pot that was sitting on the cooker.

'Mostly,' I told her.

'*Mostly?*'

I nodded. 'What you havin' for dinner?' I asked, changing the subject.

'Goulash.'

I smiled. Sophie's mum stirred the stew and then came over and sat down again. She put her hand on mine and sighed.

'It's not getting any easier, is it,' she said, not really asking a question.

'No . . . but there's something I have to talk to you about . . .'

'What?'

I shook my head. 'When Stephen comes downstairs,' I said.

She picked up the newspaper, looked at the story about the missing teenager for a moment and then folded it shut.

'So many stories,' she said absent-mindedly, before scratching at her scalp underneath her hat.

Year 9

24 October

Jit's email, 17.35pm:
that joke ain't funny.

Sophie's email, 17.50pm:
my – what a lengthy and witty riposte. you've sure got a way with words.

Jit's email, 17.58pm:
switch 2 msn – this is shit.

Sophie says:
God – that took ages – well ok – maybe only five mins but you get my point. I had to ask my dad for help. he was well annoyed – hee hee! still here I am – what can I do for you?

Jit says:
you was the one wanted to chat

Sophie says:
it's a good thing you're so cute. what was so bad about the joke?

Jit says:
what joke?

Sophie says:
the one in the email???? are you smoking weed or something?

Jit says:
nah – just tryin to chat to a nex person too

Sophie says:
you really know how to make a girl feel appreciated. see you at school.

Jit says:
only joking!!!!!!!!

Soph01 is offline.

Three

Sophie's dad walked into the kitchen and sat down, smiling at me. He was wearing a pair of black trousers with a white shirt, tucked into them. His hair, as always, was immaculate.

'Hey, Jit.'

'Mr Davis . . .'

He gave me a funny look and asked me the same thing as his wife had at the door. 'Since when did you start calling me—?'

'Dunno,' I replied, cutting him off.

Stephen shook his head and picked up the newspaper I'd been looking at earlier. 'There's a story in this – about another . . . er . . . young woman,' he began.

'Jit saw it,' Imogen told him.

'Why have you been ringing things in it?' I asked, turning the mug of coffee I was holding round in my hands.

'I really don't know,' replied Stephen. 'It feels like I'm doing something maybe – like trying to get some-where . . .'

'I don't understand . . .'

He looked away and then back at me and there

were tears in his eyes. He put the paper back down on the table before he spoke, folding it neatly in half. 'She's out there somewhere and I want to find her – that's what I keep telling myself – and I need to be doing something. I just thought I might find similarities between this girl's disappearance and Sophie's . . .'

I thought about how close Stephen and Sophie had always been. The way he had doted on her, sometimes so much that I'd felt annoyed and jealous. And I realized how wrong I had been – to think that way. Now I just felt bad for him. For both her parents.

'That's just silly,' commented Imogen.

'I know,' agreed Stephen. 'It's just that I . . . I don't know what else to do.'

'The police told us that she may never come back. We have to come to terms with that – we have to.'

'*No!*'

Only the shout hadn't come from Stephen – it had been me. Sophie's parents were both staring at me. I put the mug down and looked away, towards the photo of Sophie and Jenna. 'She is coming back,' I told them.

'Jit . . .' said Imogen.

'She is – that's what I wanted to talk to you about,' I continued.

'Is there something . . .? Do you know something?' demanded Stephen, his face lighting up for a second and his left eye twitching ever so slightly.

I shook my head. 'Just what you already know. The emails and the text messages that I told the police about . . .'

'So what are you on about then?' asked Imogen.

I gulped down air and looked straight at her. 'I'm going to find her,' I told them both. 'I'm gonna contact some of the girls who were with her at that festival and ask them what happened and see if I can—'

'*Jit!*'

I jumped slightly because I'd never heard Imogen shout like that. She looked at me with real anger and then burst into tears, running out of the room. Stephen let her go, not responding at all.

'I'm sorry, Stephen . . .'

'It's OK – she's still really sensitive and I don't think that'll change until we find out what happened . . . er . . . if she's . . . er . . .'

'Let me try,' I asked him.

'*Try?*'

'To find her – I know you think the same way as me. She's not dead.'

Stephen flinched at the word 'dead'. He looked at the newspaper and then at the ceiling. His eye twitched again, this time uncontrollably.

'What are you going to do that the police can't?' he said, asking me something that I'd been asking myself over and over again.

'I don't know but I gotta try,' I replied. 'I can't sleep, I can't work – nothing . . . I have to try . . . I . . .'

I wanted to try and explain what was going on in my head: the way Sophie and me had argued before she went. That last text message I'd received, the one that I hadn't told them about. And that song – playing over in my head – reminding me of the pact we'd made with each other. I wanted to explain it all, but by then I was out in the pounding rain and running up the street, crying and feeling ashamed.

Four

Sophie went missing at a music festival the summer after we left school. She'd been planning to go with Jenna for nearly the whole year before. During our GCSEs they had been emailing and messaging a couple of other girls they'd met in a chatroom, getting all excited. Two weeks after we'd broken up for the holidays, Sophie had called me to tell me that she was going to the festival with Jenna and two other girls, Louisa and Hannah.

After hitching a ride in a van with an Australian guy, they'd hooked up with a group of eight or ten others at the festival. Sophie had sent me three texts that day, telling me all about it and saying she wished I was there. But we'd already fallen out and I only replied once, a short, sullen message that to this day I regret sending.

The next message I got from her had come the following morning and then another around lunch time. A third one came through at four in the afternoon, telling me that she was worried about two of the men they'd hooked up with. By six pm the messages were frantic, telling me to call her parents. Something was wrong but she didn't have time to tell me properly. The messages were short and quick. And each time I tried to call her back her phone just rang and rang, not even going through to the answer service. At the same time I couldn't get hold of Sophie's parents and Jenna's phone was turned off or had no signal. I was going mad, desperately trying to get in touch with someone – *anyone*.

By nine in the evening I was still trying to get in touch with her parents: Imogen's phone was off and Stephen was away on business and no one was answering their landline either. In the end I managed to get through to Stephen and told him what was going on. But by then it was too late. From what Jenna told the police and us later on, Sophie had already gone. Taken off with a group of people who Jenna described as weird.

'Like one of those cults,' she'd told me, sitting in Leicester's Victoria Park, in front of De Montfort Hall, watching people walk by.

'A cult?'

She'd shaken her head. 'Maybe not a cult exactly, but strange. They called everyone brother and sister and one of them, this tall, ugly blond bloke, kept on asking if we knew about the final reckoning.'

'Did you tell the police all this?' I asked stupidly.

'Of course I did, Jit. Why wouldn't I?'

'I was just asking,' I replied – it was a stupid question.

'I feel sick,' Jenna told me.

'Me too.'

* * *

18

The following morning, a Sunday, I got a text from a girl called Claire, telling me that Sophie was fine and that she didn't want me to contact her again. Ever. At the time I was so angry that I threw my phone at my bedroom wall and broke it. But the police, who became involved during the following week, managed to salvage the data on it and saw all the messages. Not that it helped. There was no response from Sophie or Claire's phones. They tried for six months to find Sophie but it was no good. It was like she'd been taken to another planet.

Three weeks after the text message from the girl called Claire, I got another, this time from Sophie. A message that made me cry like a baby. But that one I didn't tell the police about.

Now, as I sat in my parents' lounge, dripping wet from running home in the pouring rain, I wondered about that last message. Why I hadn't told the police and whether it might have helped. What it meant and why she had sent it, after everything she'd said just before she left. The front door opened and shut and broke into my thoughts. It was my mum.

'What the hell are you doing?' she demanded.

'Got wet,' I told her.

'And that's why you're sitting on my leather sofa, is it?'

'Sorry . . .'

My mum looked at me with concern and pity. 'Go and get changed and towel off your hair, Jit. You'll catch a chill.'

'In a minute,' I replied.

She came and sat down beside me, knowing what I was thinking about. 'It will get better,' she said, trying to comfort me. But it was a lie and she knew it. It was never going to get better and I told her so.

'So you're gonna just sit around and let your life go to waste?' she asked me.

'I don't care . . .'

'Well I do, so get your arse up off that sofa and sort yourself out!' she shouted.

'Get lost!'

My mum's mouth opened and closed slowly. I could see that she was fighting two emotions. Rage and sympathy. In the end sympathy won out.

'Go and get changed, Jit, and I'll make you something to eat,' she said in a soft voice.

I looked away from her gaze. 'I'm sorry, Mum.'

'So am I, Jit – so am I.'

Stephen rang me about an hour later.

'I'm sitting here listening to some music,' he told me. 'Lester Young.'

'Oh . . . me too. Isn't he the guy that worked with Billie Holiday?'

'You've got a good memory,' replied Stephen.

'Nah – Sophie just brainwashed me with your music collection, that's all.'

'Imogen's gone out.'

'You want me to come back round?' I asked.

'If you can bear it. I'm sorry about before but I

can't understand why you ran off,' he told me.

'I don't know why either,' I replied honestly. 'It was like the walls and the ceiling were closing in on me. I couldn't breathe . . .'

'Just get back over here. There's something I want to say to you.'

'About what?' I asked, sitting up on my bed.

'Sophie.'

'What about her?'

There was a silence on the line for a few moments.

'I was thinking about it. If you want to try to find her then how can we stop you? I could tell you and tell you that it won't do any good but you're not going to listen, are you?'

'No.'

'So I thought that maybe I could *help* you . . .'

'*How?*' I asked.

'I don't know, Jit. We could plan something – a strategy . . . Maybe I could give you some money.'

'I don't want your dough,' I told him.

'For *her*,' he replied. 'I don't know where you're planning on going but maybe it will help you get there.'

I didn't say anything. Instead I wondered whether Stephen knew about Sophie's song too. But then I decided that I was being stupid – of course he hadn't said 'get there' because of the song. Sophie was close to her dad but that song – the pact we'd made around it – that was ours alone. I was sure of it.

'Jit?'

21

'I'm here.'

'So are you coming round?'

'I'll see you in fifteen minutes,' I told him.

'I could come and pick you up if you like. It's raining buckets.'

'I like the rain,' I said, before hanging up.

Year 9

6 November

Sophie says:
you're such a geek! the way you were sucking up to mr turner.

Jit says:
get lost! anyways he's my footie coach and I like him.

Sophie says:
whatever! so what about sharon in 9tm? you fancy her or what?

Jit says:
er . . . NAH!!!!!!!!!!!!!!!!!!

Sophie says:
there's no need to be mean about it. what's the prob anyway? you'll get a snog out of it . . .

Jit says:
you like her so much you snog her.

Sophie says:
ehh!!!!!!!!! i don't do lezzer or hadn't you noticed?

Jit says:

i ain't seen you with no lads – mayb you is lezzer.

Sophie says:

what's with the delayed response, young man? were you looking up how to spell maybe, maybe?

Jit says:

huh?

Sophie says:

oh never mind. i'm not a lezzer – although there's nothing wrong with being one!

Jit says:

oh right – i had to take a piss and is a good job there's nothing wrong with it cos you is one!

Sophie says:

JIT!!!!!!!!!!!! that's disgusting. i don't need to know when you go to the little boy's room.

Jit says:

you asked. and stop changing the subject, soph.

Sophie says:

what subject?

Jit says:

the lads thing. how come I ain't seen you with no lads an that?

Sophie says:
saving myself for you, can't you tell? laugh out loud!!!!!!!!

Jit says:
really?

Sophie says:
in yer dreams boy – lol!

Jit says:
oh.

Sophie says:
don't be like that I was only

jitrai01 has signed out.

Five

'Where are you going to start?' asked Stephen. I shrugged. 'I thought I'd speak to Jenna again and see if she has any ideas,' I replied.

Stephen opened and shut a book by James Ellroy lying on the kitchen table.

'That's a mad book,' I said, taking a swig from the can of lager I'd been given.

'*American Tabloid*? I've read many reviews of it – none of them called it mad,' he teased, smiling at me.

'You know what I mean . . .'

'Yes – I do,' he agreed, picking up the book and putting it down again.

'So yeah – I'll talk to her and see what happens,' I said.

'Who?'

I shook my head and smiled. 'You need to get some new memory. Yer old one's done a runner.'

Stephen shrugged this time. 'Work is really busy . . .'

'Still travelling all over the place?' I asked, although I knew he was.

He nodded. 'I'm in Newcastle from tomorrow for two days and then it's straight on to Copenhagen.'

'Nice . . .'

He smirked. 'Not when you're so tired that all you get to see is the hotel room and the breakfast in the morning.'

'I wouldn't complain,' I told him.

'You'd better get yourself a job in software then,' he replied, getting up and walking over to the sink.

'Nah — that shit is too exciting. I was thinking maybe rock star or actor — something everyday. Run of the mill . . .'

Stephen turned on the cold tap and held his hands underneath it, letting the water cascade over his fingers. I didn't say anything and a few moments later he turned the tap off, wiped his hands on a tea towel that hung from the cupboard door under the sink and started making a cup of tea. I waited for him to speak again.

'The two girls Sophie and Jenna went to the festival with — they live in Leicestershire, don't they?' he said finally as he stood with his back to the worktop, holding his tea.

'Loughborough and Melton — why?'

'I just wondered if they would be a good place to start.'

'Might be,' I agreed.

'That's what the police did . . .'

I flicked the edge of the table with a nail. 'Who cares what they did — it wasn't enough!' I replied angrily.

'Jit . . .'

'It's true — if they'd done their jobs she'd be here now.'

It was five minutes before either of us spoke again and in that time I got a text from Jenna, telling me that she was in O-Bar on Braunstone Gate. I sent her a reply, saying that I'd be there in an hour.

'I'm gonna go see Jenna in a bit,' I said, breaking the silence.

'Are you going to ask her about—?'

'Yes,' I interrupted.

'Good. Just let me know what you're going to do and I'll sort out some money for you.'

I shrugged. 'I can use the old banger my dad's got parked in our drive – so it'd just be petrol an' that. Like I said – I don't want yer money . . .'

'What kind of car is it?' he asked.

'R-reg Golf – it's OK.'

'Great cars – built to last . . .' he began but he didn't finish what he was saying. The sentence just kind of withered and died.

'Can I ask you a favour?' I said.

'Yes . . .'

I gulped down air, wondering if he'd think that my request was a bit odd. When I'd stopped swallowing air I looked straight at him, watching his eye start to twitch.

'Can I have a look at Sophie's bedroom?'

He looked away and then picked up the James Ellroy novel again. Handing it to me, he nodded. 'And put that back in there too – on her bookshelf. She'll miss it when she gets home otherwise . . .' he said.

'Yeah – I know . . . her and her books . . .' I tried

28

to smile but it probably came out as a grimace.

'What are you looking for?' he asked.

'Nothing really,' I said truthfully. 'I just wanted to . . .'

This time *my* sentence died prematurely on my lips.

'I don't even know why I asked,' he admitted. '*I'm* always in there . . . Go ahead and then I'll drop you off at Jenna's.'

'She's right over the other side of town,' I told him, 'in a bar on Brauny Gate.'

'I don't mind – I need to get some cigarettes and, besides, it really is pissing down now.'

I gave him a funny look. 'You don't smoke.'

'Yes I do,' he told me. 'I started again . . .'

Her bedroom was neater than I'd ever seen it. Everything had been cleaned and tidied and the piles of books that she normally had lying around the foot of her low bed had been placed on their shelves. There was a fresh white towel hanging over her chair and her desk was arranged the way she liked, with the keyboard sitting exactly fifteen centimetres in front of her TFT screen, with the mouse on the left, not the right. I closed the door behind me and stood just inside, taking the space in. The smell and the feel of it.

After a few minutes I walked over to her bed and sat down next to one of the pillows. I could smell her perfume, which her mum had obviously sprayed recently, and thought back to all the time we had spent in her room after we'd got to know each other. The teasing and the laughter and the messing about. I thought again about the time she'd looked at my eyebrows and then pulled out her tweezers.

'Time for some deforestation!' she'd said to me.

'You what? You crazy or summat?' I'd said in reply.

'Oh, quit being such a girl,' she answered, jumping on me and pinning me down in one lightning-quick move.

I smiled as I remembered how I hadn't put up a fight and had just let her pluck my eyebrows, even when she'd accidentally plucked a piece of skin off too. The warmth of her body, so close to mine, the heat making my cheeks burn and my heart pound. The way her breath smelled, like cherries, and the weight of her breasts against my chest when she leaned across me to get a tissue and wipe away the droplet of blood above my right eye . . .

Twenty minutes later I went downstairs and told Stephen I was ready to go.

Six

I watched Jenna go up to the bar with the tenner I'd just given her. She was odd-looking but in the best way. So small and skinny that you could easily lose her in a crowd, but really pretty, with sharp features and kind of electric-blue eyes. And the mad shock of spiky blonde hair that sometimes made her look like a kid's puppet. She was wearing mashed-up trainers, low-slung jeans, a red slim-fit T-shirt and an old black Carhartt hoodie, and as she walked back with our beers I watched some of the men she passed looking at her. One in particular, a tall, gangly wannabe gangsta, grabbed at her, getting a mouthful of abuse for his trouble. He said something in reply, and as she came and sat down he turned to his mates and started laughing.

'He botherin' you?' I asked stupidly.

'He can bollocks . . .' she replied. 'What is he anyway – Bollywood meets Snoop Dogg?'

'Thinks he is,' I said, staring in his direction until he looked back.

I heard Jenna say, 'Leave it, Jit,' as I shrugged at the lad and then put my bottle down on the table. Ready to go over to him.

'He's only about fifteen anyway,' she told me, putting her hand on my thigh, a barrier between my temper and trouble; a temper that had always been bad and had only got worse since Sophie disappeared.

'He's a fuckin' knob!' I spat, finally taking a swig of my lager.

'Will you just calm down . . . ? I thought you wanted to talk about summat? I gave up a date with a really cute snowboarder to meet you.'

I looked at her and then burst into laughter. 'Yeah, right! This boarder – did he bring his own snow?' I asked.

'He obviously weren't snowboarding when I saw him,' she replied.

'Which was when?'

'Last night – I was in Nomad,' she told me.

'You're always out . . .'

We spent another twenty minutes or so having a go at each other before I said I wanted another drink.

'Me too,' said Jenna. 'And I wanna know why I'm here.'

'It's a date,' I told her. 'I'm just waiting for my jeans to sag down off my arse and for my snowboard to arrive.'

She swore at me. At the bar I got served quickly and I turned with two bottles of lager in one hand, only to be faced with the gangsta wannabe.

'You was looking at sumt'ing earlier – what?' he asked me in a high-pitched voice.

'Yer mama,' I said, before attempting to walk away.

Wannabe stood in my way, got all up in my face, as his hip-hop heroes probably said.

'You wanna watch it, bro – I'll merk a bwoi fe fun . . .'

'You what?' I asked. 'What the hell are you talking about?'

'Just watch yer back, innit,' he said, before smirking and walking back to his mates.

I let him go and walked back over to Jenna, who was smiling at me.

'I'm proud of you,' she told me. 'Twelve months ago you would have done your nut over shit like that – you been to anger management?'

I put the beers down. 'Summat like that,' I replied. 'I failed the class though . . .'

With that I walked over to Wannabe and punched him in the back of his head. He lurched forward, sending a table crashing. Someone screamed, someone punched me in the side and then, when Wannabe turned to face me, I dropped two kicks on him. One in his balls and one under his chin. Wannabe's world went black as I felt myself being lifted almost off my feet and dragged out. I let it all happen, retreating into myself as the world turned in all around me. Sophie's song turned over in my mind . . .

'You're a dickhead,' Jenna told me. We were sitting in her bedroom an hour or so later.

I didn't say anything. Instead I let her continue to call me names and tell me off. When she'd finished I stood up and walked over to the window, pulling the curtains to one side.

'What you doing – spying on the neighbours?'

'Just looking,' I replied. 'I spoke to Sophie's dad earlier . . .'

Jenna tugged at the ring in her bottom lip with her tongue.

'About trying to find her,' I added. I let the curtain fall back and turned to her. 'He thinks it's a good idea.'

'But the police never found her – what makes you think that you—?' she began.

'It's just a feeling,' I replied, cutting her off and then regretting it.

'Yeah – it's called stupidity,' she said, lying back on her bed so that her feet were resting on a pillow.

'I can't explain it – I just know that there's more to it . . .'

Jenna sighed and turned on her side, propping her head up. 'Look – don't take this the wrong way – but we all know how much you liked her and—'

'It's got nothing to do with that,' I barked.

'Jit . . .'

'I'm sorry . . . but it isn't because I love her or anything. We made a promise to each other . . .'

Jenna nodded. 'The song – yeah, I know.'

'She told you?' I asked in amazement.

I had always thought that it had been just our thing, that song. Not that it mattered that much. Without Sophie there was no pact and the song didn't mean as

34

much as it had. That was why I was so desperate to go and find her. That and something else. Something deeper.

'She told me most things, Jit. We *were* best friends . . .'

'But—'

Jenna grinned. 'She told me about your hairy arse too,' she teased.

'But—'

'Oh shut up, Jit. You sound demented. *But, but, but, but!*'

A memory began to form in my mind. Spring, during Year 10, with Sophie round at my house, waiting for me to get ready to go into town. Me, getting out of the shower and going into my room. Sophie knocking on the door. Me not hearing her knock because my music was too loud. Sophie walking in, just as I was picking up my boxer shorts . . .

'It *was* funny,' I said to Jenna, snapping back into the present.

'I can imagine,' she said, rolling over onto her front.

'You want me to go?' I asked.

'No – I want you to tell me what you want,' she said, picking at her lip ring again.

'I need to know what happened again – exactly like you remember it,' I replied.

The look in her eyes told me that I'd given her the wrong answer but I ignored it. Instead I walked over to her desk and picked up a pen and a notepad.

'You mind if I use these?' I asked.

'You mind if I get drunk?' she replied.

It took her no more than a minute to leap up from her bed, run downstairs, return with a bottle of tequila and take up exactly the same position that she'd vacated sixty seconds earlier.

'Shoot,' she said to me, before swigging from the bottle like an alcoholic.

It took Jenna about half an hour to go through her memories of the festival, and all the way through it she continually apologized for not taking more care of Sophie.

'It was this boy, Carl,' she explained. 'I bumped into him randomly in the queue for a food stall. He was so cute and he wouldn't stop talking to me. He was with a completely different group of people – that's why I wasn't with Sophie and the other lot we met as much as I should have been – I was so—'

'It's OK,' I reassured her. 'You didn't know that she was going to disappear.'

'But I should have been with her,' she replied.

'Where did you go and what time?' I asked.

'I dunno – it was during the Saturday morning . . . Carl asked me to go and check out some of the stalls with him. I told Soph that I was going and she said it was OK. She was with Louisa and Jamie, the guy who'd given us a lift to the festival . . .'

'And your phone went dead?'

Jenna nodded, a guilty look crossing her face. She shrugged. 'I forgot to take my charger with me.'

'Which explains why I couldn't get hold of you.'

'Yeah . . .'

'So how long was it before you found out about Sophie?' I asked.

Jenna went red.

'*Jenna?*'

'Not until the next day,' she admitted. 'I stayed with Carl. His mate had a van and we spent the night there . . . When no one knew where Sophie was the next day, I went mad trying to find her. I looked everywhere . . .'

I nodded as she explained, a small part of me slightly angry even though she wasn't telling me anything I didn't know already and I had no right to feel that way. Jenna had just been enjoying herself. Nothing that had happened was her fault.

'You can't imagine how much I wish I could go back and change things,' she said.

'I think I can,' I countered. 'That's all I think about . . .'

This time Jenna nodded. 'And I never really noticed Shining Moon, the leader of the cult, apart from a couple of times. He was weird – that's all I thought – and Carl and his mates were ripping the piss out of the cult.'

'What about the girls you went down there with and the other people you met – did you speak to anyone else much?'

'Same thing,' she added. 'I spoke to them, sure, but I wasn't that bothered. I was just so into Carl – I know it sounds silly but—'

'No it doesn't,' I told her, before remembering the text I'd received from the girl called Claire. I asked Jenna if she knew her.

'No – I didn't meet anyone called Claire. Honestly, Jit – I wish I could tell you more but I spent my time with Carl and I was drunk and smoking bud and . . .'

It was then that the tears started to flow down her face. I stopped asking her questions and gave her a hug. She didn't stop crying though. Not for long while.

The next morning I rang Sophie's dad on his mobile as I walked home, slowly and shakily, thankful that it was a Saturday. Jenna had found some more tequila the night before – another half-bottle – which we'd also battered before passing out. I'd woken up with her feet in my face and left her where she was, semi-naked and totally unconscious, thankful that her mum was away with her boyfriend.

'Call round later and pick up the money I've got for you,' Stephen told me.

'I can't,' I replied. 'Can you post it through my door?'

'Erm . . . it's rather a lot of cash – what if your parents open it?' he asked.

'They won't,' I told him. 'They'd never open my mail. Can you do that then?'

'Yes . . . Are you OK, Jit? You sound ill.'

'Late night,' I said, stopping to let my head come to a standstill. I felt sick.

'So where are you going first?'

'Jenna's calling the girl in Loughborough later.'

'So you're going today?'

I shook my head, which was a ridiculous thing to do. It's not like he could see me.

'Jit . . . ?'

'Yeah – sorry. We're going tomorrow.'

'Why not tonight?' asked Stephen as I approached a row of houses with big front gardens and loads of bushes.

'Got summat on tonight . . .' I managed to squeeze out, wondering why he sounded so impatient, which was stupid really. It *was* his daughter I was trying to find.

'OK – let me know. I gotta run,' said Stephen.

'Yeah,' I replied, snapping my phone shut, turning and puking into the biggest bush I could find.

He entered the room, listening to the floorboards creaking beneath his feet. Reassured by their sound. The screaming had subsided a few minutes earlier, washing away the fear like rain, washing away the heat of a scorching day. Now he felt strong, in control. The way he wanted to be. He held on to the plastic bag with a grip so tight that the veins in his hand felt as if they would pop.

The chest freezer was in the corner, double padlocked. A treasure chest. His collection. He walked over to it, set the bag down on the floor and searched his pockets for the keys. The first key on one ring, the second on another. Both of them kept in separate places. Secret places where no one would find them. Removing both padlocks, he set them down next to the bag and opened up the freezer, the heavy, hinged lid squeaking.

He looked down at his collection and smiled to himself. Not even a shudder this time. He was in control. Control. Only no sooner had he said the word out loud for the second time than the shuddering began. It began in his gut, deep down where he held all the fear, and it made him double over. He began to sob, to howl. They were coming . . .

He sat down next to the bag and tried to catch them in his throat, send them back to where they had come from. But it would have been easier to stop a jet fighter. One, then two, then dozens of screams poured out of him like gushing water, until he was on all fours, retching and coughing and wondering whether his stomach might fall out of his mouth. The sweat broke cold on his forehead. Sensing that he was nearing some point of no return, he grabbed the bag, used the side of the freezer to steady himself and pulled his latest treasure out. He held it up to the light, smiled through the pain and kissed it on its cold, hard lips.

Then he let it fall in amongst the others . . .

Seven

Hannah, one of the girls Sophie and Jenna had travelled to the festival with, lived in Loughborough and Jenna told me that she'd agreed to meet us in a bar near the town centre. I wanted to find out what she and the other girl, Louisa, knew. Jenna came round at just gone seven in the evening and my mum let her in, bringing her into the kitchen.

'Jit – your friend is here for you.'

'Hey, Jenna,' I said, smiling. 'You want a drink or summat?'

'I'm OK, thanks,' she replied, winking at me when my mum wasn't looking.

'So what time does the film start?' I asked her.

'Eightish,' she lied, remembering what I'd said to her on the phone earlier in the day so that we could take the car.

'Have you got your driving licence?' asked my mum.

'No – who carries them around?'

'Jit . . .'

'Mum, I've been driving since I was fifteen, thanks to Dad – practising on that strip of land he bought.'

'That's not the point—' she began.

'Yes it is. I had four lessons before I passed my test. We'll be fine.'

Jenna went a bit red and looked down at the floor. I gave my mum a look.

'See?' I said to her. 'You've embarrassed my friend because you're embarrassing me. She didn't come round here to listen to you talking to me like I'm some kind of kid.'

My mum smirked. 'Oh, she's fine,' she told me, winking at Jenna.

'Well *I'm* embarrassed,' I told her.

'*And* you look like death,' she pointed out. 'Your cheeks look green.'

'Don't feel too well,' I said. 'Maybe I'm coming down with the flu or summat.'

'Or maybe it's all the booze you were drinking last night?' she said slyly.

'I wasn't that drunk,' I protested.

'You came home at half-ten in the morning with vomit on your clothes . . .'

Jenna looked at me and then giggled. 'Lightweight – you never told me you'd been sick!'

'Just don't drink anything tonight,' warned my mum.

I nodded. 'I ain't stupid, Mum,' I replied, before turning to Jenna. 'Come on – let's get out of here before she thinks of summat else we can't do.'

In the car Jenna pulled a CD out of her bag. I looked at it, then at her.

'*And . . . ?*' I asked.

'Music for the trip,' she said, smiling sweetly.

'It's only fifteen minutes up the road,' I pointed out. 'We ain't on no road trip.'

'Not yet,' replied Jenna. 'But you never know – I even brought clean underwear and a toothbrush.'

'Sounds to me like you've got a pulling kit in that bag,' I said.

'Complete with weed.' She grinned at me and pulled out a spliff. 'Wanna get high?'

I shook my head and pulled out of the drive, pushing her CD into the player. A skateboarder rock band came blaring out of the speakers.

We headed across the city through Belgrave before turning onto the A6 and the two pulls that I had on Jenna's spliff were making my head spin. At one point I thought about pulling over but by the time we'd reached Rothley I was fine, just a bit light-headed. Jenna didn't say a word until we were five miles from Loughborough.

'Do you know the town centre?' she asked me.

Through the fug that was crowding my brain I said no and looked out of the window at fields. My mind spun backwards in time to when I was seven and my dad had taken the family up to Newcastle to see relatives. Whenever I saw a cow I'd shout 'Moo!' because I thought it was really funny. By the time we made it to my uncle's house, my old man was going mental, telling me that he was going to stick me up a cow's bum if I didn't stop. I was thinking about it when Jenna's voice cut through the memory.

'Jit!'

'Huh?'

'You're mashed!' she squealed, giggling like a child.

'Nah! Just thinking, that's all,' I protested.

'About what?'

'Cows and things,' I said before I could stop myself.

'See? You're gone,' she said.

I took one more look out of the window and saw a herd of nine or ten cows. My dad's voice echoed around the space in my head and I looked away suddenly, not even knowing why.

'When we get into the town just follow the signs to the centre,' Jenna told me.

'Yeah . . .'

'We're meeting her at a bar called Polaris or something . . .'

I gave her a funny look. 'You don't even know where we're goin'?'

She shrugged. 'It's about the size of your back garden. We can't get lost.'

An hour later we were driving in circles around Loughborough, passing the same shops and signs over and over.

'Left!' shouted Jenna, ten metres after we'd passed the turning.

'Er . . . give me a bit of notice and I might stand half a chance,' I replied.

'Stupid boy.'

'Oh shut up – let's just stop an' ask somebody,' I suggested.

'Yeah – him over there,' she agreed, nodding at a lad in a baseball cap and Burberry coat who was heading towards us.

I pulled into the kerb, wound down my window and shouted across the street. ''Scuse me, mate!'

The lad turned to see if there was anyone else around, pointed at himself and then crossed the road to the car.

'We're lookin' for some bar – what's it called, Jenna?' I looked at her as she lit up a fag.

'Polaris,' she told him, smiling.

'Polari?' the lad asked, in an East Midlands drawl.

'P-o-l-a-r-i-s,' repeated Jenna. Slowly.

The lad shook his head. 'Ain't no Polaris round 'ere but there is a likkle bar called Polari . . .'

'Where?' I asked.

The lad smirked at me. 'See that left turn back there?' he asked.

'Yeah?'

''S down there, matey . . .'

I didn't wait for him to finish. Instead, seeing that there was no traffic in my rear-view mirror, I hit reverse and screeched backwards down the road, just as the lad shouted something that I couldn't hear.

'Burberry-wearing knob,' I said, turning into a badly lit, dingy side street.

'There it is!' Jenna told me, pointing at a small bar with a blue neon sign across the window.

'Polari,' I said.

'Maybe the S stopped working,' suggested Jenna.

'Yeah – or they can't spell in the sticks.'

'Come on – park up. I want a vodka,' she insisted. I saw a space in front of me, to the right, on double yellows. I pulled in, reversed, straightened up and turned the engine off.

'Let's go then . . .' I said, checking my back pocket to make sure I had some money.

Year 9

3 April

Soph01 has signed in − 17.59

jitrai01 sends a wink − 17.59

Sophie says:
i'm bored. whaddya doin?

Jit says:
nuttin

Sophie says:
nuttin? is that something that squirrels do when they hoard them?

Jit says:
huh?

Sophie says:
never mind. you wanna come over here?

Jit says:
yeah but me mum won't let me.

Sophie says:
is it cos i is white?

Jit says:
no – cos yous a knob.

Sophie says:
charmin. wish all the boys were as suave as you.

Jit says:
whats that mean?

Sophie says:
never mind about that. why can't you come over?

Jit says:
homework.

Sophie says:
but you're on msn

Jit says:
i know that, you know that, but me mum don't though, does she?

Sophie says:
had a dream about you.

Soph01 sends a wink.

Sophie says:
well . . . ?????????

Jit says:
well what?

Sophie says:
don't you want to know?

Jit says:
if you like . . .

Sophie says:
if i like what exactly?

Jit says:
you know what I mean.

Sophie says:
uh-uh

Jit says:
was i naked?

Sophie says:
see? you do want to know.

Jit says:
so was i?

Sophie says:
was you what?

Jit says:
naked?

Sophie says:
depends on whether dolphins wear clothes.

Jit says:
eh????????????

Sophie says:
dolphins. those things that swim the sea and do tricks – big long noses, like yours.

Jit says:
i know what a dolphin is – but why one of them?

Sophie says:
oh go on then – seeing as you're desperate to know. you were a dolphin in my dream and i was a tuna.

Jit says:
tuna? lololololololololololol!!!!!!!!!!!!!!!!!!!!!!!!!!!!!!!!!!!

Sophie says:
what's so funny about tuna?

Jit says:
matt levy calls you a fish all the time.

Sophie says:
matt – the one with the greasy hair and the red socks?

Jit says:
yeah.

Sophie says:
why?

Jit says:
cos you got them big lips – says you look like one.

Sophie says:
i'll have you know that my lips are considered sexy but you're only a boy so why would you know?

Jit says:
weren't me said it – i like your lips.

Sophie says:
AHHHHHHHHHHHH!!!!!!!!!!!!!!!!!!!!!!!!!!!!! that's the sweetest thing you've ever said to me. big kiss.

Jit says:
just tell me the dream thing and stop with that nonsense.

Sophie says:
you were caught in a net and i was swimming by and i saw
you and cut you out.

Jit says:
what with?

Sophie says:
whaddya mean?

Jit says:
were you some kind of gangsta tuna or sumthing – carrying
a blade and that?

Sophie says:
i used my teeth silly!

Jit says:
then what?

Sophie says:
we went off and swam round the oceans together. having
adventures.

Jit says:
tell me 2mrw gotta go

Sophie says:
oh! why?

Jit says:
my mum wants me to do my homework.

Sophie says:
where is she?

Jit says:
standing watching me type this. bye . . . .

jitrai01 has signed out.

Eight

My mobile rang just as we were about to enter the bar. I looked at the screen and saw Stephen's name. Turning to Jenna, I handed her a tenner.

'Get me a lemonade,' I said.

She winked at me and went in.

'Hey, Stephen,' I answered when he spoke down the line.

'How's it goin', Jit?'

I watched a couple of men with skinheads and bomber jackets walk into the bar, staring them down. Neither of them gave me a second look. 'Fine,' I replied.

'Where are you?'

'Loughborough.'

'Oh – did you get the money?'

'Yeah,' I told him as a short, round girl with piercings all over her face walked past me and into the bar. While Stephen banged on about something I started wondering what kind of bar I was standing outside.

'I'll call you tomorrow,' I said as he started coughing. 'You OK?'

He coughed some more and then told me that he was fine, although his voice was a croak. 'That's what you get for taking up smoking again,' he said. 'I'll see you, Jit.'

'Yeah,' I replied, flipping my phone shut.

Inside the door was a cloakroom area that led down a corridor and towards some stairs. The walls were draped in a deep-red velvet material and the lighting was dim. There were paintings all down the corridor, on both walls. Portraits of various faces, all painted up like clowns in day-glo colours. Halfway down the corridor, a doorway led into the bar area. I walked in, looking around for Jenna.

I found her at the bar, having a conversation with some woman. As I approached she smiled at me and said something to the woman, who turned and smiled at me too. She was about six foot three and I had to look up at her. It was only then that I realized that 'she' was a 'he'.

'Hello, sweetheart − your girlfriend here has been telling me all about you,' he said, leaning over and talking into my ear.

I took a step back, nodded at him and turned to Jenna. '*Girlfriend?*' I asked.

'I was only kidding − you know, those *joke* things − supposed to make you *laugh*?' she replied, handing me my lemonade.

I took a big swig and tasted vodka. 'This has got—' I began, but Jenna cut me off.

'Oh, relax − it's only *one* drink.'

I nodded at her and turned to look around the bar, which was as dimly lit as the entrance. Towards the back of the room were a load of tables and booths, most of them empty. The two skinheads were sitting at a table to my right, facing the window to the front. They were laughing and joking with each other and, as I watched, the taller of the two reached across and kissed the other one on the mouth. Suddenly realizing what was going on, I turned to see a lesbian couple at the bar; one of them was the woman with the piercings, the other a tall, pretty girl with long brown hair.

Jenna nudged me in the back. 'Worked it out then?' she said with a sly grin.

'Yeah . . .'

'Apparently Polari is some gay language used all over the world.'

I shrugged. 'At least we know that they can spell,' I replied as the barman smiled at me.

'Oh, don't start getting all homophobic on me,' said Jenna.

'I'm not. I just wanna find this Hannah bird and get out of here.'

'You're just boring,' she told me, before downing her drink. 'Can I have another one?'

I shook my head at her. 'Not with my money.'

'Charming . . .'

She turned to the bar and ordered another drink from the ever-smiling barman, using the change from the tenner I had given her. I let it go and scanned the room again, trying to work out whether Hannah was there. I didn't have to wait too long. The tall, pretty girl smiled at me and mouthed my name. I nodded. She whispered something to her girlfriend and then came over.

'How did you know who I was?' I asked.

'Sophie showed me a photo of you – on her phone – and besides, you're with the gnome.'

'Gnome?'

She nodded towards Jenna, who was obviously ignoring Hannah. I wondered what was going on with them and made a mental note to ask Jenna.

'Forget her though,' said Hannah. 'I thought you wanted to talk about Sophie.'

The second mention of Sophie's name sent my mind off in about ten directions at once and I felt a lump growing in my throat. I urged back the tears and looked away.

Hannah touched my forearm. 'Come on,' she said. 'There's a booth down the back where we can talk.'

As I followed her I wondered why Sophie had shown some random girl my picture. Was it like some indicator of how she'd really felt? Maybe she'd been slagging me off, calling me a wanker because we'd fallen out. And then I remembered her last text to me, telling me how much she loved me and how she had made a big mistake, letting me go. My heart started to thump in my chest and my vision blurred. As I sat down there were beads of sweat forming at my hairline, tickling my forehead and scalp. I wiped them away with my forearm and looked at Hannah.

'So what do you want to know?' she asked in her posh accent.

'Just stuff, I guess.'

'I'll tell you what I told the gnome over the phone,' she replied. 'The police asked me about a million questions last year and then they came back in February and asked me some more. I don't know anything about where she went – I just know who she was with at the festival.'

I eyed her suspiciously. 'Who?'

Hannah shrugged and watched me light a cigarette before telling me that she didn't like smoke.

'Why didn't you say something before I lit it?' I asked, mashing the fag out.

'Dunno,' she told me. I got the feeling that she didn't like me. Not that I cared. The only thing I wanted from her was her take on the people who had been with Sophie at the music festival, and maybe some more ideas about who to speak to.

'So who was she with?' I asked again, looking at the wasted cigarette in the ashtray and wondering if her story would match what Jenna had told me.

'A load of us,' Hannah told me. 'Louisa, Jamie, a few other girls who I didn't know.'

'What about someone called Claire?' I asked.

Hannah thought about it for a moment before shaking her head. 'I didn't meet anyone called Claire and I generally notice the girls . . .'

She winked at me but not in a friendly way. It was more sardonic than anything else. I ignored her and moved on with my questions.

'Do you know where Jamie is?' I asked.

'That Aussie dickhead? Birmingham . . . said he was in a band . . .' She looked angry for some reason.

I looked at her. 'Why don't you like him?' I asked, taking a risk.

'Who says I don't?' she replied, looking down at the table.

'I can tell.'

'*Yes* – of *course* you can,' she sneered.

'You got an email or mobile for him?'

She opened her little handbag and pulled out a scrap of paper. 'I wrote it down for you,' she said, 'although the police know about him so I don't see what you're going to do – that they can't.'

'That's none of your business,' I told her.

'He's a dickhead,' she repeated.

'Who – Jamie?'

She nodded.

'Why?'

'That's none of your business,' she replied, annoying the hell out of me.

'Anything else?' I asked, anxious to get out of the bar.

'Yeah – one thing . . .' she said, taking a packet of cigarettes out of her handbag and lighting one. I was about to say something but stopped myself. She was trying to wind me up and I wasn't going to let her. Whatever game she was trying to play, she'd have to play it on her own.

When I didn't respond to the cigarette she told me the other thing. 'Sophie was right about you,' she said.

My ears started burning. 'Why – what did she say?' I snapped.

'That you were an obsessive little boy.' There was almost pleasure in her voice when she said it.

'Fuck you . . .'

'Well – what are you trying to prove?' she asked me. 'The police can't find her and you think you can? You're just a headcase . . .'

In my mind, little eruptions of superheated lava began to go wild and red dots danced in front of my eyes. If Hannah had been a lad I would have shoved the cigarette up her arse. But she wasn't and I didn't. Instead, as her girlfriend joined her, I stood up to leave. Hannah pulled Miss Pierced-Face towards her, groping at her tits like she'd get some kind of reaction from me. But I just let her play her game and went to find Jenna, Hannah's words turning over in my brain, again and again.

In the car I asked Jenna what her problem with Hannah was.

'She's a lying, manipulative, two-faced slag,' she spat.

'So why didn't you tell me that before I met her?'

Jenna bit her bottom lip before replying. 'Because I didn't want it to get in the way of you askin' her stuff . . . besides, what does it matter?'

'She kept on callin' you a gnome and slaggin' off the

guy called Jamie,' I told her. 'Got the impression you and her had a fallin' out an' that.'

Jenna grinned. 'At least I ain't a drama queen,' she told me. 'And she would slag Jamie off – he was tryin' it on with her and she was playin' him.'

'How'd you mean?'

'Pretendin' to like him and that. She's a stupid fucking bitch . . .'

'That bad?' I asked, grinning.

'Worse,' she replied. 'If I was like you I would have shoved her head through the table.'

'Did she get on with Sophie?' I added, ignoring her dig at me.

Jenna nodded at me. 'Hannah fancied her.'

'How do you know?' I asked.

'I just do,' she said.

'Anything else?'

'Yeah – she fell out with Louisa too.'

'Great,' I said, more to myself.

'Bitch . . .' muttered Jenna.

Year 9

5 April

Sophie says:
wanna see my humps, baby?

Jit says:
huh?

Sophie says:
my humps, my humps, my humps, my humps, my humps –
lolololol

Jit says:
you smoking crack?

Sophie says:
sorry bout that – my dad was asking me some stuff. wanted
to know who i was messaging. told him it was the pope. he
didn't look too happy. and to answer your very silly
question: no, i'm not smoking crack – i'm just playing. i'm
bored – whaddya doin?

Jit says:
homework

Sophie says:
come round – we can do it together, wink wink

Jit says:
you're mad

Sophie says:
yeah but it's a good mad

Jit says:
should be your surname lol

Sophie says:
huh?

Jit says:
likkle miss goodmad

Sophie says:
strange boy. anyway you've got twenty minutes to get your sexy bum round to mine or it expires.

Jit says:
what expires?

Sophie says:
your naughty-sophie permit.

Jit says:
huh?

Sophie says:
you coming over or what?

Jit says:
on my way x

Sophie says:
ah – a kiss? for me? you're so lovely.

jitrai01 has signed out.

Nine

The next morning Louisa sipped at her coffee in a café in Leicester town centre. She was really striking, with short dark hair and bright green eyes, and she wore no make-up at all from what I could tell. She spoke about the festival as I sat and people-watched in the mirror behind her head. An alternative world where everything was back to front. I wondered whether I had fallen into that mirror image. Whether in the real world things were like they had always been and Sophie was where she'd always been. On the end of a phone line or the Internet. And was I watching myself from the real world, scrabbling around trying to find clues about my friend? Clues that maybe didn't exist anywhere but in my head?

'She really had a thing about you,' Louisa told me.

I snapped out of my thoughts and raised an eyebrow. 'What makes you say that?' I asked.

'Just call it intuition . . .'

'According to Hannah she hated me.'

Louisa looked away as she replied. 'Hannah would

say that – she thinks she's in competition with every male in the world.'

'I don't—'

She smiled. 'The lesbian thing. It's all a game to her. She'll get bored of it soon and go back to being straight.'

'So she's not really a—'

'What she is,' Louisa told me, 'is a drama queen. Seeking attention . . .'

I gave her a funny look. 'You know a lot about her.'

'More than I'm gonna tell you,' she said, grinning.

I watched in the mirror as a couple sat down on a sofa behind us and kissed each other. Something in my heart thumped.

'So what makes you think Soph had a thing about me?'

'The way she slagged you off,' revealed Louisa. 'She spoke about you all the time I was with her.'

'But if she was slagging me off then—' I began, only for Louisa to shake her head.

'Don't play dumb. She told me how clever you are . . .'

I shrugged.

'She said you've got a hundred and thirty IQ – is that true?'

'A hundred and forty,' I admitted.

'But that's like genius level – and you sound so thick . . .'

I watched her face for a moment to see if she was joking. She was.

'It's just some stupid tests – I practised them for ages . . .'

'It's still bloody high – genius boy . . .'

I grinned at her and felt embarrassed and proud all at the same time. And then I started to talk my IQ score down.

'The tests are all different and they're like culturally biased towards the Western world,' I told her. 'And I ain't got no common sense, so what good is all that IQ if I can't read a map?'

Louisa gave me a funny look. 'You don't know how to read maps?'

I shook my head. 'That was just an example.'

'You definitely don't know how to read people,' she said.

'What makes you say that?' I asked before my supposed genius brain worked it out. 'Oh, you mean Soph . . .'

'She said that you get violent too.'

I nodded. I didn't have anything to hide. 'Sometimes – if people piss me off,' I admitted.

'Did you ever get violent with Sophie?'

I glared at her and whispered, 'Never . . .'

'Just askin' . . . I suppose the police asked you that too?'

I nodded again, watching some more people in the mirror. A pretty, dark-haired lady with a small child, a drunken bum looking for the toilet, two Japanese students, a man so fat that his mass fell down round the sides of the chair he'd taken, making it almost disappear.

'Anyway, what is it you want to know? I ain't got all day. And shouldn't you be in college or something'

'Can't be arsed,' I told her.

I thought about everything I had been told so far and began by asking her about the Australian man, Jamie. I looked back at myself in the mirror. Sunken, hollowed eyes, pinched cheeks, shaved head. It didn't look like me. It looked like a ghost.

Back at home that evening I grabbed a pad and a pen and sat down at my desk. Louisa's words flooded back into my head and I wrote them down. The cult that Jenna had mentioned was not really a cult, according to Louisa. More a collection of nutters with pretensions. Same for the tall, ugly blond man who Jenna had told me about − Shining Moon. Louisa said he was the leader of the group and went on about the final reckoning, which she'd laughed at, right in his face.

'Funnily enough, he stopped talking to me after that,' she'd said, smiling.

She'd told me that the 'cult' was based in the north-east of Scotland, between Edinburgh and Aberdeen, in a farmhouse that belonged to Shining Moon.

'How'd you know that?' I'd asked her.

'He told me. Before I upset him by laughing at his stupid theories. Invited me to join him there whenever I wanted to. Like, yeah − that's gonna happen . . .'

'You got an address for it?'

She'd shaken her head and suggested maybe he'd given it to one of the other people they had been hanging around with. I asked about the last time she'd seen Sophie.

'Lunch time on the second day – the Saturday.'

'She sent me a text in the afternoon. Something about some dodgy men . . .' I told her.

'Could have been anyone. There were loads of dodgy men about – talking all kinds of shit.'

'What kind of festival *was* it?' I'd asked.

'The music bits were great but there was all this weird new-age shit around the edges. Crystals and mysticism. Stuff like that. I just avoided it – most of those people needed a good wash.'

'Did you meet anyone called Claire?' I asked. 'I got a text from her – telling me that Sophie didn't want to hear from me again.'

'When was that?' she asked, looking puzzled.

'The day after she went missing – the Sunday. Why?'

'I didn't meet anyone called Claire but there were a load of people around that I kind of know. We met up with them on the Friday. I don't think there was anyone with them called Claire.'

'I tried calling this Claire's number back,' I told her. 'But the phone was switched off . . .'

'That's strange,' she replied. 'Did the police check her out?'

'I think so,' I said. 'I told them about the text from her. Could she have been part of the cult?'

'I dunno – there were some women with them so it's possible but I just don't know. Like I said – after my run-in with Shining Moon I left them to it.'

* * *

I started thinking about some of the other people Sophie had been with at the festival. There was Jamie, who was working in a bar called Orbit in central Birmingham. I pulled two pieces of paper out of my pockets and looked at them. One had Jamie's email address, which Hannah had given me. The other had his mobile number and actual address, from Louisa. I wrote the information down, balled up the two pieces of paper and flicked them in the general direction of my waste-paper basket. Halfway towards their intended destination they split apart and went their separate ways.

And then I started to compare the pieces of paper with Sophie and me – flying off in different directions – and I started to get angry . . .

I brought my mind back to the present and continued with my list: there was a Kiwi bloke called Ritter – his surname according to Louisa, who had no idea how to contact him. A girl called Anna, who lived in Streatham, who Jenna had given me a number for. And a list of names and places with no other details. David from Newcastle, Micky in Edinburgh. And Claire, who none of the people I'd spoken to so far knew anything about. I finished and looked back through what I'd written, wondering where to go next and deciding quickly that it should be Jamie. Then I turned on my PC and clicked on the iTunes logo on my desktop, finding Sophie's song in the online music store. I downloaded it, sat back and listened to it, on repeat, with tears in my eyes . . .

Ten

J amie rang me back two days later. I had a free afternoon and I was clearing out our loft. I had dust in
my eyes and up my nose and when I answered my
mobile I sneezed before saying anything else. Jamie
laughed down the line.

'Never been greeted with that one before,' he said in
a broad Aussie accent.

I said sorry and sat back on the floor, pushing a box
that held some old school stuff away with my feet.

'You wanted to talk to me about Sophie?' he asked
on the other end of the line.

'Yeah – she was my friend . . .' I began, wondering
what to tell him. It didn't take long. 'Me and her dad
are trying to find her,' I added.

'Oh right, mate. Only I spoke to the police about it
ages ago. Got the impression that she was . . . y'know
. . . er . . .'

'I know,' I told him, nodding my head. 'We're just
trying one last time. Maybe the police missed something or—'

'Well, whatever I can help you with . . . She was a
nice girl, that one.'

I could hear in his voice that he wasn't just saying it to make me feel better. He really meant it and that made me like him instantly. But then I wondered whether he might be the person who had taken her and I was on my guard again.

'Could we like meet up or summat?' I asked him.

'Sure, mate. I'm always at the bar apart from Sunday evenings – the Orbit.'

'How about later on today?'

'Sure . . . I'm startin' work around six,' he told me.

I brought up a mental image of the other names I'd written down after speaking to Louisa.

'There was a bloke from New Zealand with you . . . Ritter?' I began.

'What – Ritter? Yeah, he was there.'

'Do you know where he is now?' I asked.

Jamie laughed. 'Ritter? If I know that mad Kiwi bastard he'll be on a board somewhere, riding the surf . . .'

I ran through potential surfing spots in my head, all of them in the UK. None of them were right though, as I found out when I pressed Jamie.

'Nah, mate – he's back home.'

'Can you get in touch with him . . . like by email or something?'

Jamie didn't reply for a moment and while I was waiting I opened the cardboard box at my feet to find a folder with Sophie's name printed on it right at the top. Something strange happened to my throat then –

like it was being squeezed from the inside – and I gasped for breath.

'You OK, mate?' asked Jamie.

'Er . . . yeah,' I said, after clearing my throat a few times. 'I'm in the loft and it's dusty. Just got to my throat, that's all.'

'Ritter didn't really leave an address, mate. He's not the type of guy that does that, if you know what I mean. Never in one place for long enough.'

'Shit . . .'

'But I might know a man who knows a man, if you get my drift. Come over later and I'll see what I can do for you.'

I thanked him and told him I'd see him at seven, memorizing the address he gave for the bar. Not that I had a clue where it was. I didn't know Birmingham at all. I put my phone back in my pocket and pulled the cardboard box closer, taking out the folder and placing it to one side. I knew what else was in the box but I couldn't see it anywhere. Finally, after removing three-quarters of the contents, I found it.

The piece of paper was crinkly and faded and I opened it carefully, making sure that I didn't rip it. Then I read what was written on it. Sophie's first ever note to me, asking me if I fancied a snog. It was in her old style of handwriting too, a style that she changed in Year 10 to something more mature, as she'd put it. At the time I'd thought she was bit mad but now I could see that the writing was childish, with swirls and little love hearts and stuff. But I liked it that way. It was hers.

'You OK, Jit?' asked my mum, popping her head through the loft hatch and nearly making me shit my pants.

'Mum!'

'Oh, who did you think it would be? And what are you doing here at this time anyway?'

I shrugged. 'No lessons this afternoon.'

'What's that you're holding?' she asked, eyeing the note.

'It was the first thing Sophie ever gave to me,' I told her, trying not to let her see how upset I was.

'Do you want me to leave you alone for a while?' she added.

I nodded like I used to do when I was a small child. I'd fall over and cut myself and she'd offer me ice cream. Through the tears and stuck-out bottom lip I'd nod, just like I was doing now. Just like a child.

I met Stephen in town at four, after I'd made a note of everything that Jamie had told me on the phone, no matter how trivial. Stephen told me he was taking a few days off work to be with Imogen, who'd had a bit of a breakdown. But when I saw him walking towards me, just outside the town hall, I wondered whether it had been *him* who'd had the breakdown, not his wife. One of my favourite words when I was younger had been 'dishevelled' – I don't know why – and it was the perfect word to describe how Sophie's dad was looking. He had a few days' stubble on his chin and his hair was wild; greasy and lying in strands on his head. His trousers had stains on them and his jacket looked like an elephant had used it to wipe its arse. And when he spoke his breath was so rancid that I had to take a step backwards, bumping into some little rudeboy as I did so.

'Watch it . . . fool!' the lad snapped.

I remembered something Jenna had said to me and thought about a baby's smile instead of smashing the lad's head against the limestone block wall of the town hall.

Stephen smiled and asked me if I'd eaten anything. I shook my head and then turned down the offer of a McDonald's. Instead we went to a Caffè Nero on Market Street. Stephen definitely needed a coffee by the look of him and I was feeling a bit tired too. I told him to get me a double shot of espresso and grabbed four sachets of sugar, all for myself. If that didn't wake me up, nothing would. In the end it was sitting down that woke me up. I didn't see the water spilled on the seat and I felt it soak through my jeans when I sat down.

'Oh for fuck's sake!' I shouted at no one, grabbing a few serviettes and trying to dry my jeans.

Stephen sat down a minute later and grinned when I told him what had happened. Then he took a pack of cigarettes out of his pocket and lit the first of about eight that he chain-smoked as we talked. On his fourth I took one too, only mine I put out after three drags. Stephen dragged each of his down to the filter, and every time he stubbed one out I saw how grubby his hands were. The filth under his fingernails. In the end I made a joke of it.

'You been sleepin' in the park or summat?'

He gave me a quizzical look and then realized that I was staring at his hands. 'Oh – no, I was doing some gardening and then I came straight here. Forgot to wash my hands, obviously . . .'

I grinned. 'No need to be defensive, Stephen. I was only joking . . .'

He nodded at me and then took a sip of his coffee, which seemed to be made entirely out of milk. I watched him spark up again and decided that I'd rather not be there any more. He was obviously going through a really hard time and I didn't want him to be embarrassed in front of me. So I lied and told him that I had to meet Jenna in five minutes.

'I just wondered how things were going,' he said, not looking at me.

I knew straight away that he'd sussed my lie but I still wasn't going to admit to it. It was the done thing anyway, not mentioning it when both people in a conversation know that one of them had just lied to get out of something. The British way . . .

'I'm in touch with an Aussie bloke—'

'Jamie,' said Stephen.

'How'd you know . . . ?' I began, before I realized. 'I guess you got to find out most of what the police did . . .'

'Exactly – which is information you can ask me about at any time. I just want you to find my daughter . . .'

I had to look away when he said the last word. His eye started to twitch and there were tears on his cheeks.

'I know it sounds crazy, Jit . . . I know. But I can feel her. She's out there; I know it and I'll never stop looking. Never . . .'

I downed my espresso in one movement before I replied, giving him a chance to compose himself. I could see why he was so dishevelled now. He *was* the one who'd had the breakdown.

'I'll do my best,' I told him. 'I promised her I'd find her if she went away . . .'

He tried to smile at me but forced smiles are always grimaces and I looked away again.

'I'll call you later, Jit,' he whispered.

And then, without a second thought or glance, he shot out of his seat and ran out of the café, forgetting his fags. I was about to chase after him when I remembered my own exit from his house a few days earlier. All I'd needed then was space to be angry and sad in. So I left him to it and lit another of his fags, wondering whether I should call Jenna and ask her to come over to Birmingham to meet Jamie with me.

Year 9

2 June

Sophie says:
hey babyface

Jit says:
who you callin baby?

Sophie says:
term of endearment??????

Jit says:
try handsome hunk then – wink wink

Sophie says:
or big headed dickhead?????lolololololololol!!!!!!!!!!!!

Jit says:
thanks for that. friend.

Sophie says:
oh dont be such a girl! what you doin?

Jit says:
homework

Sophie says:
on msn????

Jit says:
nah – i just have it on all the time in case my mates are trying to get in touch.

Sophie says:
male or female mates?

Jit says:
both – you jealous?

Sophie says:
of your skinny ass? nope – fancy a snog?

Jit says:
yes please!!!!!

Sophie says:
well you can't have one!

Jit says:
so what do you want then?

Soph01 is away.

Fifteen minutes later

Sophie says:
sorry babe – my dad wanted to ask me something – it took ages

Jit says:
thought you'd gone all mardy – what did he want?

Sophie says:
oh nothing really. he's just making sure that i'm doing all my homework. wants me to do well. and me – mardy? – with you? never. you're my little babyface.

Jit says:
do me a favour? never call me that at school. i'll get killed.

Sophie says:
you and your rep. is that why you pretend to be thick all the time?

Jit says:
no

Sophie says:
touched a nerve??? heehee

Jit says:
more like on my nerves.

Sophie says:
ooooh! toys out the pram, babyface???

Jit says:
you busy?

Sophie says:
never too busy for you, my handsome hunky babyface – lol

Jit says:
might come over in a bit. did you do that iq thing at school?

Sophie says:
yes. distinctly average i'm afraid – you?

Jit says:
er – yeah

Sophie says:
so what did you score? mine was 110 which is still high but
not genius like i really am – must have been wrong that test
– lol

Jit says:
they got mine wrong so I gotta take it again 2mrw. mr green
wants me to do another one.

Sophie says:
why?

Jit says:
cos I got 140 and they thought it was really high.

Sophie says:
OH MY GOD!! you
gotwhat??

Jit says:
140 – why?

Sophie says:
oh like nothing, babyface. that's only GENIUS level. no big
deal.

Jit says:
it ain't that big a deal – we'll see how i do on the next one.
it was probably completely wrong or summat.

Sophie says:
seriously jit do you know what that means?

Jit says:
what what means?

Sophie says:
your score, you dummy.

Jit says:
dunno but greeny was all red in the face when he saw it.

Sophie says:
it must be wrong because you're acting like a right idiot.

Jit says:
huh?

Sophie says:
look it up on the net. famous iq scores or something. you're a genius and you don't even know. i might have to marry you now.

Jit says:
eh!!!!

Sophie says:
well maybe not marry you exactly but at least a snog. then when i'm a grandma i can tell my grandchildren that i once snogged a proper genius.

Jit says:
you mean bonafide

Sophie says:
see? you're even showing off now – get your lovely little bottom round to mine pronto and i'll print off a load of stuff from the web. it's not some little thing, jit. seriously. i'm gonna go tell my dad!!!!!!!!!!!!!!!!!!!!!!

Jit says:
but i don't want you to tell your dad.

Soph01 has signed out.

Eleven

The sky started to turn orange on the horizon as I drove down the M69 with Jenna sitting next to me. Rain was lashing down at the car almost horizontally, and the spray from the rest of the traffic made it hard to see what was going on. I was still doing ninety though, amazed at how good the Golf was. It kind of purred through the gears, despite being so old, and there wasn't a rattle anywhere. I sat back in my seat and thought some more about Sophie, watching the sky darken from the steely grey it had been when we'd left Leicester.

'Looks like it might get really bad,' said Jenna, understating things.

'It *is* bad,' I replied. 'I can't even see the road, never mind the cars in front . . .'

'Slow down then.'

Twenty minutes later we were sitting in traffic on the M6 when my mobile rang. I looked at the screen and saw Stephen's name.

'You gonna get that?' asked Jenna.

'Yeah,' I told her, looking in my mirrors for any sign of the police. When I saw that none were around I answered.

'How's it going?' asked Stephen. His voice was hoarse and he coughed.

'We're in Birmingham,' I told him. 'Or at least we will be when the traffic moves . . .'

'To see the Australian chap?'

'Jamie . . . yeah.'

'And is Jenna with you?' he added.

'Er . . . yeah, she is. You wanna talk to her?' I replied.

'No – just checking,' he told me. 'Let me know how things go – if you need any more money or advice . . .'

'There is one thing – I meant to ask you before: did the police ever mention a girl called Claire?'

'Um . . . let me think. I do believe there was some-one by that name. Can I think on it and get back to you?' he asked, before going into a coughing fit.

'Yeah – I'll call you in the morning,' I said, letting him ring off and cough his guts up.

Jenna gave me a funny look. 'Who wanted to talk to me?' she asked, confused.

'No one – that was Stephen.'

'Oh,' she replied, before lighting up a fag.

'Open a window,' I told her.

'And get soaked? No thanks.'

I parked illegally down a side road off Broad Street, and once Jenna was happy with her make-up we walked back towards the bars. I didn't actually know which way Jamie's pub was but it didn't matter. At the junction we turned right and headed towards the centre of Birmingham, in the direction of the

Symphony Hall. I only knew where it was because it was signposted and Jenna started winding me up.

'You sure it's this way?' she asked, lighting yet another fag.

'You're going to end up as a fag hag,' I told her. 'You got that notebook I gave you?'

Jenna stuck her middle finger up at me and then dug into her handbag, pulling out a spiral pad. I'd written down everything I'd been told about Sophie's disappearance and somewhere in the notebook was the name of Jamie's pub. I opened it as we walked, careful not to bump into any of the crowds of people around us.

'It's rammed,' I said, to no one in particular.

'Beats the pants off our city,' replied Jenna.

I looked up just in time to sidestep two hard-looking men who were wearing suits and skinheads. I stepped to my right but one of them still barged into my shoulder. For a split second I thought about saying something but common sense kicked in and I let it go. I was stupid, not suicidal.

'They look rough,' whispered Jenna after they'd gone.

I grinned. 'Not as rough as her,' I said, nodding my head towards the other side of the street.

'That's just nasty,' agreed Jenna, looking at a big woman who was crouching in the gutter with her skirt hitched up round her waist, peeing. She was part of a hen night, and her pissed-up mates were standing on the pavement whooping and egging her on. The big woman began to shriek with laughter and then she stood up, shaking her leg and trying to grab a passing bloke.

'Fancy a shag, babs?' she asked him.

Jenna turned to me and screwed up her face. 'Dirty cow . . .'

I flipped two more pages as I shook my head and found what I was looking for. Now I remembered that the bar was called Orbit – we definitely hadn't passed it. I stopped and looked around, confused by a sudden surge of bodies walking past, drenched in perfume and aftershave, all of them talking in the Brummie accent. Feeling lost, I stepped into the road, only to be beeped by a passing car full of youths.

'I think you need to wake up,' Jenna told me. 'What are you doing anyway?'

'Trying to work out where this bar is,' I replied, wishing that Jamie had given me better directions than 'Broad Street, mate – you can't miss it.'

Jenna grinned. 'Don't be tetchy, Jit.'

'Well, have *you* seen it?' I asked, annoyed.

Jenna shrugged. 'Maybe it's the other way,' she suggested, stating the obvious.

'Shitty place,' I replied as another car full of blokes sped by, bhangra music blaring.

'Come on – I wanna drink,' she moaned.

I looked at her, felt myself getting angry and then walked off in the opposite direction.

'Jit!'

★   ★   ★

89

It took ten minutes to get to Orbit after we'd asked some lads where it was, and then the doormen wouldn't let me in because I was wearing trainers.

'We're here to see Jamie,' Jenna told them.

'Yeah?' said the bigger of the two, a bloke with short dark hair and an earring.

I watched him lift one of his meaty hands up to his face, noticing how hairy it was, just like my dad's – only the doorman was wearing three heavy-looking rings that looked like they would leave a pretty good impression on your face. If he punched you.

'Just ask him,' pleaded Jenna when I told her to leave it.

'I don't know no Jamie,' said the other one, a shorter man with blond hair and small piggy eyes that were set too far apart. He smiled at me and I noticed that he had three teeth missing.

'He's Australian,' continued Jenna. 'And we've driven over from Leicester just to see him. You have to let us in . . .'

The shorter doorman smirked at the big one. 'Show us yer tits then,' he said to Jenna.

'Oh, piss off!' she snapped, just as a third man walked out of the bar and asked what was going on. This one was younger and better dressed and I assumed he was the manager because he was holding a bunch of keys.

'We're here to see Jamie,' I told him. 'He asked us to come over . . .'

'And they won't let us in,' added Jenna.

90

I pulled her arm and she gave me a fiery look but got the message to leave it alone.

'Wait here,' said the younger man. 'I'll go and ask him.'

As he stepped back into the bar I looked at the doormen but they had totally lost interest in us. Instead they were checking out the hen party we had seen earlier. I pulled Jenna to one side and told her to calm down.

'You're tellin' *me* to calm down?' she asked, looking amazed.

'There's no point in causing grief on the door. Then we really won't get in.'

She bit her bottom lip before replying. 'But he just asked me to show him my tits!'

'Forget about it – he's a dickhead.'

I turned to see if the doormen had heard me, but they were chatting up the hen party.

'See?' I said to Jenna. 'He's not even bothered. Forget it . . .'

She was about to go mad when the younger man came out, shaking his keys in his left hand.

'In you go then,' he said to me with a wink. 'Jamie's over by the bar.'

'Cheers, mate,' I replied, smiling.

The man leaned towards me and grinned. 'Them doormen are idiots,' he said. 'Don't worry about it, kid.'

I wondered whether he knew that Jenna and I were underage and didn't care. Or whether he had no idea.

In the end it didn't matter. He was getting us into the bar and that was all that counted. All I wanted to do was speak to Jamie, find out what he knew and get back to Leicester.

Twelve

'That Hannah's a freaky one, isn't she?' said Jamie, picking up his bottle of Coke and taking a swig. 'You can say that again,' I replied.

We were sitting facing each other at the bar, on stools with red leather seats. The place was empty apart from a group of girls in one corner and a couple sitting by the window. Jenna was standing a couple of metres away from me, talking to someone on her mobile and drinking vodka and Coke through a straw. The stainless steel bar was about six metres long, and on the wall behind it were hundreds of bottles of booze, all backlit in oranges and reds, with a stainless-steel backdrop.

'It's OK in here,' I heard myself say, although my mind was racing through what Jamie might be able to tell me: Jenna had said she'd left Sophie with Jamie and Louisa. Did he see who Sophie went off with? Were there any other people that Jenna and the others might not have seen? Like Claire, maybe?

'Pays the bills,' he replied.

'Huh?'

'This place . . . You OK, mate?'

I nodded. 'Just thinking,' I told him.

'Must be hard on you – being so close to Sophie and all . . .'

I just looked at him and didn't say anything. Instead I started seeing Sophie's face in my head and then I had a flashback to her hurt look when I walked out on her the last time we'd been together. I gulped down air as my stomach started to somersault.

'So whaddya wanna know?' he asked.

'Huh?'

'You sure you're OK, mate?'

I nodded again. 'Just a bit under the weather,' I replied.

'Not surprised in this country. You wanna go out to Oz, mate – six months of sunshine and you'll be right.'

I picked up my notebook, which was on the bar next to my pint of lager, and opened it. Then I put it back down, pulled out my fags and lit one. I took two long drags before grabbing my notes again.

'Tell me about Shining Moon,' I said.

'That bloke? He's a real drongo, mate.'

I looked up at Jamie and started grinning.

'What?' he asked me, confused.

'I didn't think Aussies really said that.'

'Said what?'

'Drongo,' I told him. 'Thought that just happened in *Neighbours*.'

'This Aussie says it,' he replied, grinning back. 'He was a right dickhead anyway . . . loved himself.'

'That's what the others told me . . . Is he like the head of some cult or summat?'

Jamie shook his head. 'Nah – from what I got he's just a rich kid playin' at bein' some kind of wizard or something.'

'Did he talk to Sophie much?'

'You know,' said Jamie, before pausing to take a swig of Coke, 'the police asked me that. Is he like the prime candidate?'

I shook my head. 'I dunno. I don't know what the police think but I do know that they've taken eight months and ain't found out shit.'

Jamie glanced down at his bottle. 'Don't take this the wrong way, mate, but what makes you think you stand a chance if they didn't find her?'

I shrugged. 'I'm not sure that I do,' I said honestly. 'I just can't sit around and do nothing any more – that's all.'

He nodded his head, waiting for me to continue.

'It's just something we said to each other . . . once – about coming to look for each other if one of us ever went away,' I added. 'It was sort of a joke but since she went it's all I've got . . .'

'You must really love her,' said Jamie.

I shrugged, feeling my cheeks begin to burn, and looked away.

'I'm sorry,' he said, sensing my embarrassment. 'What else do you wanna know?'

I looked round at Jenna, who was still on her phone, and then down at my notes. 'I spoke to Louisa—'

'She's a nice girl,' he interrupted.

'Yeah . . . anyway she said that there were loads of new-age types all over the place.'

Jamie nodded. 'Yeah – there always are at that festival. They burn effigies and play with crystals and stuff.'

'Any of them look strange to you?'

He laughed. 'All of 'em, mate.'

'Yeah – Jenna said summat about them being weird. She also said that she left Sophie with you, the last time she saw her.'

'I was with her around lunch time,' he said. 'Me and Ritter – but not for that long . . . After that I dunno what happened to her . . .'

'Yeah. What about this Ritter?'

'Ritter? Back over on the other side of the world, like I told you on the phone.'

'Did you get a contact for him?'

'Yeah – here . . . I wrote it down.'

He handed me a beer mat that he'd pulled from his hooded top. I looked at it and saw an email for Ritter and a phone number.

'What's the number?'

'His mum's place. In Melbourne – she's an Aussie like me. He goes and hangs out there sometimes . . . At least that's what he told me. To be honest I only met him a few months before the festival, mate. We met up because we were both going there but I don't actually know that much about him. And you'll have a hell of a job getting hold of him, mate. He's always on the go.'

'Did you tell the police about him?'

'Yeah – but they didn't seem too bothered. I told them that we left the festival together and then he went

96

on down to London with some girls. Besides, the only name I had for him was Ritter. Like I told you – I don't know that much about him . . .' Jamie shrugged.

'Anything else you can think of that might be important?' I asked.

'Nothing that the others can't tell you. Give me yer number and if I remember anything I can always buzz you.'

'What about someone called Claire? I got a text from her on the Sunday morning – about Sophie. Did you meet her?'

'Claire? Yeah – there *was* a Claire – short blonde girl with bright blue eyes . . . She was workin' on a stall. Selling candles and carvings and shit.'

My eyes lit up and I scribbled down what he was telling me. 'Do you know how to contact her?' I asked excitedly.

'Some shop in Covent Garden. London. Said she worked there in the week. She was a babe, mate.'

'Do you know which shop?'

'Yeah,' he said, grinning. 'Hard to forget the name – it's so stupid.'

'What is it?' I asked, sensing the impatience rising within me.

'Candles and Things,' he replied. 'Silly name . . .'

'Sounds kinda apt to me,' I replied.

'Yeah – I suppose so,' he said. 'But you'd think they'd come up with summat more original or inventive, wouldn't ya?'

I nodded.

'Anyone else, mate?' he asked.

I looked through my notes and checked on the other names with him as Jenna came and joined us, saying hello to Jamie, ordering another drink and pulling up a stool. When I was done asking him some more questions and checking what he knew with Jenna's story he told us he had to get back to work. I looked at Jenna and asked her what she wanted to do next.

'Dunno,' she replied. 'Head back home? I've got some really nice weed.'

I thanked Jamie and told him I'd be in touch before following Jenna out of the bar.

'You didn't say much to him,' I said to her as we found the street the car was parked on.

'Don't really know him,' she told me.

'But weren't you all at the festival together?'

'Yeah – but I didn't speak to him really . . . I was more interested in his mate, Joey – before I met Carl, that is . . . Besides, he was too busy chatting up that bitch Hannah. I spoke to him a bit in the car when he gave us the lift down there, but not much after that. I don't think he was interested in me.'

I stopped in my tracks, running through my notes in my head. 'Who's Joey?'

'Oh . . . that's Ritter's name.'

'Did you tell the police that?' I asked. 'Only Jamie reckons he only knew him as Ritter.'

'Yeah, I did – but I saw Joey on the evening Sophie went missing and he wasn't with her so the police didn't seem that interested.'

I made a mental note of what she'd told me as I started to walk again, wondering if it could be significant that the police hadn't bothered with Joey Ritter. What if he'd been the one who had taken Sophie – or seen the person who had? I pulled out the beer mat that Jamie had given me and called the number on it. The phone on the other end rang and rang but no one replied. I hung up and only then did I wonder about the time difference between the UK and Australia.

'Who you calling?' asked Jenna.

'I thought I'd try Ritter,' I replied. 'No reply . . .'

Jenna nodded at me.

The car was parked under a streetlamp and as we approached I saw two things that made me curse. The first was a pile of puke that someone had left by the rear driver's-side tyre. The second was the fixed penalty notice that some bored wanker of a copper had stuck to the windshield.

'Great . . .' I said, pulling the ticket off and fighting back the urge to smash my hand through the glass.

As I stood and looked at the ticket three women walked past and one of them gave me an intense look. She was short, about five feet nothing, and her face was chiselled. She looked like an ancient Egyptian goddess, with feline eyes and bee-stung lips. For a moment I was lost in her face, staring. Then reality kicked in and I looked away, embarrassed. When I looked back a moment later she smiled and asked me if I was OK. I nodded and searched hard for something to say, but by then she was gone. I watched her walk away, hips swaying, and realized that her lips reminded me of Sophie's. So much so that I suddenly felt like I wanted to scream.

The music was turned down so low that he could barely make it out. Not that it mattered. All he wanted was to hear her pick up the phone. Just once and he'd be on it in a flash, talking to her, his latest angel, perhaps the penultimate one . . .

When she didn't answer after five minutes of redialling, he picked up the phone and looked at it over and over. Hit the menu button and scrolled down to the gallery. Opened the images file, pressing select when he saw her face. Set it as his wallpaper. Sat and stared at it for what seemed like an age.

But it was only ten minutes. And still no reply. He put the phone down, picked it up and put it down again, anger coursing through his veins instead of blood. Rich, deep crimson anger from the most hidden part of his heart. He picked up the phone once more, looked at her picture. The blonde hair, the blue eyes . . .

Ten minutes later he found himself fingering the cardboard container that had held his Big Mac. He pushed the lid down, flicked it up, pushed it down again. Where was she? Why wasn't she answering? Is this what it means, he asked himself, to be in love?

Not like before, with the others. That was love that died. This time it would be eternal, live on for ever . . .

Two hours later he watched her as she walked into her house and shut the door. A hallway light came on and went off in the instant it takes to flick a switch up and down. He waited a heartbeat longer and then crossed the road and vaulted the fence that led to her garden. Three months he'd been watching her. Even in the pitch-black night he knew every step, avoided every obstacle, found the ladder. He placed it gently against the wall and let desire carry him up to her window. He tried to shut off his mind, to purify the moment that was to come.

She'd left a gap in the curtains again as she stood with her back to him, removing her vest top and jeans. He steadied himself as she looked at herself in the mirror and wiped make-up from her face, something he'd wanted her to do from the start. Such intrinsic beauty needed no mask. Not until the time was right. As he let his mind wander, she removed her underwear and slid into her bed. His eyes began to water and behind them a hammer struck down on the nerves. Feeling himself go light-headed, he made his way back to the ground and out of the garden to his car. She was the perfect addition. Perfect. Smiling for the first time in a week, he started the engine, engaged gear, shot the handbrake to the floor and pulled off. Twenty-five minutes and he'd be able to see his angel collection again . . .

Thirteen

I came back from college at lunch time again, made myself a cup of coffee and sat on my bed writing down everything Jamie had told me – which didn't seem to be very much. Then I went through all my notes, over and over again, hoping that something would leap off the pages and give me an idea of what I was doing and where I was going. I wanted to find Sophie but I didn't know if I could. Self-doubt began to creep into my head as I questioned myself again and again. What did I think I was doing? Considering I was supposed to be so intelligent, I was acting like an idiot. Did I really think I would have any luck finding Sophie when the police hadn't? I had no chance.

But even as I was telling myself that I was going round in circles, that nothing good would come from what I was doing, a little voice in my head told me to carry on. I don't know what it was – a gut feeling or an instinct – but somewhere in my notes, somewhere out in the big wide world, there was someone who knew what had happened to her. Someone who had seen her being taken away. Someone who had hurt her or killed her. Someone. And my head was telling me that the answers lay with Claire – the girl who had sent me the text.

When I looked at my clock I saw it was three o'clock. I swore out loud and jumped off my bed. I'd arranged to meet some mates in town and I was late. But the first thing I did was to try Ritter's mum's number again. No reply and no answering machine. Fifteen minutes later I was sitting in a coffee shop listening to my mate Azhar banging on about girls and music. I was looking out of the window, waiting for another mate, Jeff, to show up. Only Jeff ran on an Antiguan clock – or so he told me – which basically meant that he was always late and couldn't give a shit about it. I looked down at my phone and then carried on staring at passers-by.

'Nah! Check the ass on dat!' shouted Azhar excitedly.

'Who?' I asked as he pointed out a blonde girl in tight boot-cut jeans and a vest top, and I immediately thought of Sophie.

'Them ting look like they was painted on,' he added, grinning like a dick.

I shrugged.

'You shit the bed or what?' I heard a booming voice from behind me.

I turned to see Jeff standing with a tray in his hands. 'What's that?' I asked him.

'More coffee – seein' as you two are sitting there with an espresso between you.'

I nodded and lit a fag.

104

'Man's quiet today,' Azhar told Jeff, talking about me.

I watched Jeff give Azhar a look that said *Hush yer mout', bwoi.*

'I'm fine,' I told them. 'Just got stuff on my mind . . .'

They both knew I was thinking about Sophie and left it at that, asking me whether I was going out that week or not.

'We could check out that Lounge place later,' I suggested. 'I could do with a beer.'

'You drivin'?' asked Azhar.

'Nope. So you can either get the bus into town or take yer two-litre foot,' I replied.

'Harsh . . .'

'Like yer mamma,' added Jeff.

I watched another blonde girl walk past the window, and as the other two drank coffee and talked shit I went over my notes again, this time in my head. The Claire thing was definitely important. I just had to find out about her. And I wasn't going to do that sitting around drinking coffee. But then I hadn't seen my two best friends for ages and I couldn't just go home. I would have felt bad. So instead I wandered around town with them, doing what thousands of bored teenagers did all over the country, before heading back to the same coffee place and staring all over again.

Life when I was out with my friends was like a slow-motion replay, with the same conversations, the same coffee in the same seats, the same girls and the same streets. Boring and slow and the perfect time to think about things. Only what I needed was to stop thinking because it was driving me insane. Or maybe that was just the boredom I was feeling, in addition to the overload of information I was being assaulted with everywhere I turned. My mobile phone, the TV, the web, posters on walls, adverts on benches, people carrying boards advertising sandwich shops and language schools, little children with dirty mouths, crying and being sworn at by their teenage mothers, cars blasting out music, road signs every metre, phone boxes that no one but immigrants and drunks used, covered in call charge information and telling you to send a text for more money than it would cost from your own mobile. And that was all from my seat in one coffee shop, in one town, in one part of the country.

And when I'd stopped thinking all that random stuff my brain was pounding and we were walking around again, avoiding stupid little shits in baseball caps and even stupider big shits with screw-faced expressions and steroid-enhanced biceps.

Back at home; back in my room, back with my notes, I made a decision to call one of the other people from the list. I did this as Jenna sat on my bed, skinned up and smoked. My parents had gone away for a few days, down to see some mad aunt in Southall. I had my window wide open to get rid of the smoke and I told Jenna to go and stand by it.

'They won't know,' she insisted. 'And, besides, don't you like having a sexy little minx lying on your bed?'

As she finished her sentence I noticed that her top, which was small anyway, had ridden up over her stomach. Something in my head told me to stop looking but I couldn't. I looked at her skin, the indentations between her ribs, the piece of shrapnel in her belly button. But then she started blowing smoke rings and I told her to stop.

'You're no fun any more!'

I ignored her and turned on my laptop, ready to send out some emails and then ring a few people.

'Fancy goin' to London for a day?' I asked Jenna.

'Yeah!'

'What was that about me not being fun any more?' I added, teasing her.

'I didn't mean it – honest. It must have been the herb talking.' She grinned at me for a few moments and then her expression changed and she bit her bottom lip and tugged at the ring in it with her tongue.

'What's up?' I asked, knowing what her new expression meant.

'I can't – got no money.'

'Spent it all on that shit,' I said.

She nodded.

I smiled. 'No problem. I'm payin' . . . well, actually Sophie's dad is but it's the same thing.'

She looked at me and shook her head. 'And there I was thinking that you were taking me out for the day. Not Sophie . . .'

I started to say something but Jenna stood up, went over to the window, docked the spliff against the outer sill and told me she was getting some water.

'But . . .'

Only she didn't hear me because she was already out the door. I smiled to myself, not really knowing why, and then sent an email to some of the people on my list, asking them in turn to forward it to their address books. I also attached a photo of Sophie that had been taken a month before she disappeared. Underneath it I put a few basic details about her and my own email and phone number. I knew it was a long shot but I didn't want to miss any chance that someone, some-where, might have a clue to her whereabouts. Once that was done, and Jenna had retaken her spot on my bed, I grabbed my parents' phone and rang the number for a girl called Anna in London. She answered on the third ring and I went quickly into who I was and why I was calling her.

'Anything you need,' she said to me when I asked if she could help.

'Thanks.'

'Don't thank me – I really liked . . . er . . . like Sophie. I was gutted when I found out.'

'There's loads of questions I want to ask you but I thought I might come down and see you or summat?'

I waited for her to give me a load of excuses, the pessimist in me coming right out, but she just asked me what I was doing the next day.

'Not a lot – I can miss college no problem. It's nearly the end of term anyway. Why, can we do it tomorrow?'

Anna giggled and told me she didn't know me well

enough and for a second I didn't get what she was on about. When I did I shrugged it off and asked where she wanted to meet and at what time.

'I'm working from eight tomorrow evening . . . We could meet up at five if you like . . .'

'That's great . . . I'm bringing another friend too – Jenna.'

'Oh, yeah – I remember her . . . spiky hair, lip ring, always got a fag?'

I laughed. 'Yeah, that's her.'

'You get into St Pants, don't you?' she asked.

'Where?'

'St Pancras station.'

'Yeah,' I told her.

'I'll meet you there. Can you get in for five?'

'We'll be there earlier than that. I need to go and check on something. But we can meet you back there at five if you like,' I replied.

'What do you need to check on?' she asked.

'Actually it's something you can help me with. I'm looking for a girl called Claire. Did you meet anyone by that name at the festival?'

'Don't think so,' she told me straight away. 'I'll have a think about it and let you know tomorrow but it doesn't ring any bells.'

'OK – see you tomorrow.'

'Great – see you then.'

I thanked her and rang off, turning to Jenna, who was looking more confused than normal.

'Claire?' she asked.

'Yeah – the one that sent me that text. I told you about her,' I replied.

'Yeah, I know that. But how do you know where she is?'

'Jamie remembered her – said she worked for some shop in Covent Garden.'

'Oh – you think she's important?'

'Yeah – I got the text on the Sunday, the day after Sophie went missing – she has to know something . . .' I said.

'But wouldn't the police have spoken to her already?'

I nodded. 'Yeah – like that means shit. They spoke to everyone. I'm just double checking, that's all.'

Jenna nodded and then grinned at me. 'What did Anna say about me?' she asked.

I grinned back. 'Oh . . . nothin',' I lied.

'You stupid shit – what did she say!' Jenna half shouted.

I shook my head and she jumped on me, trying to tickle it out of me, and for a while I forgot all about Sophie.

Year 10

15 October

Sophie says:
hey my favourite young man – what you doin'?

Jit says:
homework. u?

Sophie says:
same. i'm bored.

Jit says:
ur always bored.

Sophie says:
did you get that mp3 i sent?

Jit says:
yeah – what's that about then?

Sophie says:
got it off my mum. dad put it onto the pc for me. great song isn't it?

Jit says:
s ok. who are the band? never heard of them.

Sophie says:
one of my mum's – yargo. they only did two albums i think.

Jit says:
and?

Sophie says:
and I thought of you when i heard that song. you are my best male friend in the whole world.

Jit says:
so if you had to get a plane or a boat to come see me you would?

Sophie says:
yes. anywhere, anytime baby.

Jit says:
but it's like a love song.

Sophie says:
i suppose it is. don't get any ideas though.

Jit says:
you wouldn't let me. but you were jealous when i went out with that nicola.

Sophie says:
oh grow up you idiot. i just didn't think she was right for you that's all.

Jit says:
yeah right. lololololololol

Sophie says:
you can be a right wanker sometimes. c u 2mrw.

Soph01 has signed out.

Jit's note, 16 October (excerpt):

. . . and it wasn't meant to be mean or nothing. I was just joking. I don't want to lose my best friend over a joke. Please don't be mardy with me. I'm sorry. Honestly . . .

Sophie's note, 17 October (excerpt):

. . . now that you've reverted back to the stone age with these notes. I know you didn't mean it and I don't know what came over me. I do care about you, Jit — I really do — and that girl was an idiot. You said so yourself. I thought part of being friends was to make sure that you looked after each other and that was all I was trying to do. Honestly. I do have feelings for you — I won't lie —but we're better off as friends. I don't ever stay friends with the lads I go out with and I value you as a friend too much to let you see what a horrible cow I am when I'm involved. Can't we just go back to being friends? I mean, it's not that I don't

think you're cute or anything. You're the cutest
boy in the whole school — it's just that . . .

Jit's email – sent 17 October @ 18.42 (excerpt):

. . . and I won't pretend that I don't like you but I get your
point so you don't have to worry about me or anything. I'll
be fine. I'll see you 2mrw at school. Bye.

Soph01 sends jitrai01 a wink on MSN @ 18.46.

jitrai01 has signed out.

Fourteen

I spent most of the night thinking about Claire. It was a big lead – that much I was sure about. She had sent me a text on the Sunday morning after Sophie had gone missing, which meant one of two things. Either she was still at the festival with Sophie, which was less likely because Jenna had looked everywhere for Sophie that day; or she was with whoever had taken Sophie – the cult maybe. The second possibility was hammering against my brain, telling me to wake up. Claire had to be important. Had to be.

Sometime around eleven p.m. I remembered that I'd told Stephen I'd call him earlier. I swore at myself and picked up the phone. He answered on the second ring.

'What happened?' he asked breathlessly.

'Nothing,' I replied. 'I just got caught up doing other stuff. Did you think about what I asked you?'

He coughed for a bit and then told me he had.

'*So . . . ?*'

'The Claire from the investigation . . . The police never spoke to her.'

My heart somersaulted in my chest. 'Why not?' I asked hurriedly.

'Because they never found her, Jit,' replied Stephen, sounding all mysterious.

'What do you mean they never *found* her?'

'The girl they were looking for disappeared too,' he added.

My heart flipped twice and I had to stand up. Rushes of nervous energy made my head spin. Two girls disappearing at the same festival? How could that happen and not make headline news?

'But there was nothing in the media,' I told him, 'nothing at all . . . when all the stuff about Sophie came out. Surely they would have mentioned it?'

'Not necessarily,' he corrected. 'I spoke to the detective in charge of the case today. Apparently this Claire girl went missing from home three weeks before the festival. Just disappeared into thin air. Then she resurfaced at the festival before vanishing again.'

'Yeah – I get that,' I replied. 'But why wasn't she mentioned in the media reports about Sophie?'

'Because the police kept her name out of it,' he told me. 'They had some promising information to follow and they didn't want to jeopardize the case.'

I thought about that for a minute.

'You still there, Jit?' Stephen asked after a while.

'Yeah – I don't get it though. They must have known that Claire was the most important witness because of that text message I got.'

'Yes – but they were carrying on two investigations and they wanted to keep them separate. Besides, Sophie didn't go missing three weeks prior to the festival. It was only when we reported Sophie missing and when you told them about that text message from Claire that they made any link. Then they—'

'Fucked up?' I asked. 'That's what they did, isn't it?'

I could feel myself getting angrier and angrier. In the end I controlled my breathing to try and put out the fire that was raging in my head. It worked.

'The Aussie bloke, Jamie, he met this Claire.'

'Are you sure it was the same one?' asked Stephen.

'I dunno,' I admitted, 'but she's the only Claire I've come up with. I'm going to look for her in London tomorrow.'

'You've got an address for her?' he asked, sounding excited.

'Only where she worked,' I said. 'And I'm assuming the police went there. What was her surname?'

As soon as I'd asked the question I felt bad. I'd talked about Claire in the past tense – did I think she was dead? I must do.

'Burrows,' he told me. 'I checked with the detective.'

'OK – I'll let you know what happens,' I replied, suddenly wanting to end the conversation.

'I'll have my phone on all the time. Call me whenever you like.'

'No problem,' I said.

Jenna rang me at two in the morning, crying her eyes out.

'What's the matter, babe?' I asked her, my voice soft and calm.

'Sophie . . .' she said, through the tears.

'What about her, Jen?'

I gave her a few moments to compose herself, listening and not saying anything. When she was ready, she told me.

'I feel guilty,' she began. 'If I hadn't been chatting up some boy . . . if I'd made sure that my phone's battery was charged . . . maybe she would still be with us.'

'Jenna—' I began. It wasn't the first time I'd heard Jenna say things like this over the last eight months.

'No, Jit! It's my fault. I was thinking about myself – drooling over some lad. I should have kept an eye on her . . .'

'But she isn't a baby,' I told her, trying to make her see sense. 'She didn't need you to keep an eye on her – it's not your fault.'

'Yes it is . . . When I charged up my phone there were fourteen missed calls from her, Jit. Fourteen. I should have helped her. I should have had my phone charged. What kind of friend does that make me?'

'Her best friend,' I replied. 'She knew it too. Come on, Jen. This is silly. You can't blame yourself for some freak thing that happened. Sophie's been taken. We don't know who took her but it wasn't you, was it?'

Through fresh tears, she said no.

'You see?' I continued. 'It's not your fault – how could it be?'

'Can you come over?' she asked.

'Jenna . . .'

'Just for a while? Please, Jit . . .'

I thought about it, wondered whether it was the right thing to do and then relented, thankful that my parents were away. No awkward questions about where I was going.

'OK,' I told her. 'But it's late so I'm only stopping for an hour – no longer.'

In the end I didn't get to bed until five in the morning and I had planned to be up by seven. I wanted to get to London early and spend as much time as possible finding out about Claire Burrows. By seven a.m. I was at my PC, searching the Internet for stories relating to Claire's disappearance. They were easy to come by – the BBC website's news archive had three reports in the local south-east news pages, two soon after she was reported missing; the third dated one week before the festival, a follow-up story that talked about how she was still missing. I read through all three and found nothing that helped me in any way, apart from allowing me to see what she looked like. They also told me which school she had attended – Burntwood in Tooting – and that her mother worked as a manager for the local branch of Marks and Spencer's, which I guessed was also in Tooting.

Then I turned to three or four newspaper websites and read through what they had on Claire too. Again, nothing major hit me – just the photos of her. She was the spitting image of Sophie. Slightly different hair maybe, and not quite as beautiful, but she had the same bright blue eyes and full lips. I sat and stared at one of the photos for a long time before something hit me. I went back to the search engine and typed in the name Kylie Simmons, the girl whose name Stephen had ringed in the newspaper.

The picture that came up told me all I needed to know. Kylie Simmons looked almost identical to Sophie too. The same eyes and lips. I felt my heart grow cold. Was there a connection between all three of them? A serial kidnapper or killer going after girls that looked almost like sisters? Just to make sure I searched for other stories about missing girls in the months on either side of Sophie's disappearance. Girls who were around the same age. I felt slightly stupid as I did so, wondering who I thought I was. Loads of stories came up, most of them about runaways who had come back home or been found, alive and well.

I ignored the stories with happy endings and concentrated on seven that were still ongoing investigations. But this time only one of the missing girls had any kind of resemblance at all to Sophie and the others. Suddenly my hunch didn't seem so great. I put it to the back of my mind, printed off a couple of pictures of Claire Burrows to show Jenna and then logged off.

Whatever was going on, I decided as I had another cup of coffee, the fact remained that Claire Burrows was the key. If I could somehow find her, or find out what had happened to her, it would bring me closer to Sophie. I was sure of that. I rang Jenna after finishing my drink. She sounded tired but told me that she'd be at the train station by nine.

Fifteen

We took the Northern Line southbound from King's Cross and got off at Tooting Broadway. The sky had turned slate-grey, making it feel as though it was late afternoon rather than late morning. Big droplets of rain were hitting the pavement, but only intermittently – as though the clouds were constipated. I looked around at the hustle and bustle of busy South London streets while Jenna lit a fag.

'Why do you smoke so much?' I asked her, watching a homeless old man with cotton-wool hair walk past, the stench of body odour making my nostrils burn.

'Why not?' she replied, shrugging.

'Fag hag . . .'

'Dickhead . . .'

'Let's go find this school,' I said.

She gave me one of her funny looks and dropped her half-smoked cigarette on the ground.

'So you wanna just walk up to some school and ask the kids if they knew Claire Burrows?'

I nodded.

'That's just stupid. Even if we're lucky enough to find someone that knew her – won't it look a bit dodgy?'

I shook my head. 'Not if you're with me. I can't just go asking questions to schoolgirls on my own – that would be dodgy.'

'Why just the girls?' she asked.

'Because it's a single-sex school,' I reminded her. 'I *did* tell you on the train.'

'And you got all this information from a load of articles on the Net?'

'Yeah – it's all there . . .'

She grinned. 'And there was me thinkin' all you did was look at porn,' she joked.

'I do that too,' I admitted. 'Now let's go before it starts pissing down.'

I looked at the *A–Z* I'd bought at St Pancras, and then at the corresponding road signs.

'This way,' I told Jenna, heading across the busy road into Garratt Lane.

The school was huge – much bigger than any school I'd ever seen – but there were only a few pupils wandering around when we reached it. Jenna hadn't stopped moaning about the twenty-minute walk and by the time we were standing by the main gates, she was red in the face.

'Five minutes, you said,' she complained.

'Oh, it weren't that far,' I replied. 'Besides, we're here now.'

'And . . . ?'

'Let's ask some questions. It's nearly twelve thirty so they must be about to come out for lunch.'

As I spoke, three pupils who looked too young to have known Claire Burrows walked across an open area between two huge buildings. They were all wearing a red, grey and white uniform and none of them gave us a second glance. I wondered what I was going to say, when and if I did say anything at all. To be honest I was having second thoughts about being there at all. It wasn't like I was going to make some magical breakthrough that the police hadn't. And thinking about that made me realize what a desperate mission I was on. If I wasn't going to find out about Claire, what the hell made me think I could find Sophie? I felt my head begin to spin and asked Jenna for a fag.

'Thought you didn't like smoking?' she asked.

'Just give ME the fucking cigarette!' I snapped, instantly wishing I hadn't.

Jenna gave me a dirty look and threw her fags at me. 'Twat . . .'

We stood there for another five minutes, not talking to each other, when a serious-looking bloke in a grey suit approached us. He had teacher written all over him.

Jenna looked at me and shrugged. 'We're gonna get shit now,' she warned.

As the man stopped to say something I looked him straight in the eye.

'Can I help you?' he asked.

'Er . . .' I began. 'Yeah, you can, maybe. I'm . . . I mean we're trying to find out about a girl who went to this school . . .'

Immediately I realized that I was being stupid. I should have just lied to him – told him to get lost. It's not like we were standing on school land. We were on the pavement.

'I'm sorry,' he said in a very serious tone, 'but any requests for information regarding our pupils are—'

'Claire Burrows,' chipped in Jenna.

I glared at her.

'Claire Burrows?' asked the man, his tone and his manner changing quickly.

'We . . . I . . .' stuttered Jenna. 'We have a friend who is missing too and we think Claire knew her . . .'

The man looked from me to Jenna. 'Have you called the police?' he asked.

I nodded. 'Our friend has been gone for eight months and the police don't know anything more than when she went missing,' I told him.

The man shrugged. 'I guess it wouldn't hurt,' he said quietly. 'What would you like to know?'

I thought hard and fast, surprised that the teacher was so willing to talk to us.

'Aren't you worried that we might be lying?' I asked.

He grinned at me. 'And why would you be doing that?' he said, exactly like a teacher. All he'd needed to do was add a 'Hmm?' to the end of his sentence.

This time I shrugged. 'Are any of Claire's close friends still at the school?' I asked.

'One or two,' he replied. 'They're in the sixth form now and I can't and won't give you their details, I'm afraid . . .'

As he answered, a group of three pupils, none of them wearing uniform, walked past us, showing a great deal of interest in our conversation.

'Off you go, girls!' said the teacher sternly.

The girls, who looked like they were my age, just laughed and walked on. I watched as they headed for the end of the road and made a note of which way they'd gone.

'What about her family?' I added, not looking at the teacher.

'I'm afraid I can't help you there either,' he replied.

'Did the police talk to the pupils after she went missing?' added Jenna.

'Yes, they did. They spoke to everyone who knew her,' he told her. 'But I'm afraid she hasn't been seen since – no reports of any kind – so I'm not sure how much use we can be to you. As a school, I mean . . .'

I noticed the change in his eyes. He was closing up for the day as far as we were concerned.

'I suggest,' he added, almost coldly, 'that you speak to the local police if you require anything more. Good day!'

And with that he walked off towards the main entrance, opening the door and going inside. Once there, he turned and looked at us, staying put until I told Jenna we were leaving.

'Well that was a waste of time,' she moaned.

'Maybe. Maybe not,' I said, walking faster. 'Come on – we've gotta find them girls . . .'

'What girls?' she asked, hurrying to keep up with me.

* * *

They were standing outside a newsagent. One of them, the tallest one, noticed us approach and said something to the other two. All three laughed, making me feel uneasy. But then the tall one smiled at me and I smiled back.

'You was askin' 'bout Claire, wasn't you?' she said as I stopped in front of her, Jenna right behind me.

I nodded.

'What are you – a journalist or summat?' asked one of the other two, a short, round girl with bright-green eyes and cornrow hair.

'Nah,' I replied. 'Me and my mate have come down from Leicester.'

'Where's that?' asked the girl with the green eyes.

'Up north, innit?' said the tall one.

The third girl looked Jenna up and down and then turned to me. 'What do you want to know about Claire for?' she asked.

'My friend has gone missing too,' I explained. 'And I think Claire might have been with her.'

'No way!' said the tall girl, shaking her head. 'Claire's dead.'

'Why do you think that?' Jenna asked.

'Been missin' for ages,' she told us. 'Gotta be dead.'

'We know someone who saw her at a music festival,' I revealed. 'Eight months ago . . .'

The girl shrugged. 'Could have been any girl called Claire,' she said, asking a question that I had been asking myself over and over. Only my gut was telling me that I was after the right girl.

'Maybe,' I said. 'Did you know her?'

'T'iefed her man, you get me?' laughed the girl with the green eyes. 'After she'd gone an' that . . .'

'Fuck off, Tash!' shouted the tall girl.

'You know it's true, Misha . . . Dat bwoi an' you was pure at it . . . from long time.'

The third girl turned to me. 'The police never found her, so how come you know she was at a festival?' she asked.

'You knew her?' I asked back.

'Yeah – she was in the year above us at school . . . she was all right . . .'

I looked at the other two and they nodded, both of them calmer now. The tall one, Misha, spoke first.

'She was nice – I knew her from baby school. It was sad what happened.'

'I don't *know* what happened,' I admitted. 'Only what I read in the papers . . .'

Misha shook her head. 'There was more to it than that. My cousin and Claire was best friends – she told me the details.'

'Like what?' I asked.

The third girl spoke up again. 'All the pupils knew it,' she told me. 'Claire was seein' some man that she met in a chatroom. Some freak – she told everyone that he was sendin' her money in the post just for stuff she was writing to him an' a few photos . . .'

I looked at Jenna, who shook her head softly.

'Did the police find that out?' she asked the girl.

'Yeah – they must have because half the kids knew. She weren't like a slag or nuffink, Claire. She was just playin' . . . didn't deserve what happened . . .'

I made a mental note of everything I'd heard.

'She said she met up with him too – said he was some high-flying business type,' added Misha.

'Really?' I asked excitedly.

She nodded. 'My cousin told the police all this stuff too – even the name the guy used in the chatroom—'

'Did she tell you?' I asked.

'Tell me what?' replied Misha.

'The name he used.'

She nodded. 'Summat freaky too. Called himself the Angel Collector.'

I nodded, my brain working overtime. I needed to know where on the Net Claire had met this man. I asked the girls.

'I don't know that much,' said Misha. 'You wanna ask the police that one.'

I smiled at her. 'Yeah, I will,' I told her, knowing that I could ask Stephen to find out more for me. 'Thanks for your help.'

'No problem,' she replied.

Jenna thanked the other two before we headed back towards Tooting Broadway.

'That was *weird*,' she said.

'What?'

'*That* . . . Don't you think it's bit strange and co-incidental that we met three girls who knew about this girl called Claire?'

'Serendipity,' I replied. 'Don't question it – just go with the flow . . .'

'Weird,' she mumbled, fishing in her pockets for a fag.

I thought about what had just happened and wondered whether any of it would help me to find Sophie. And the name of the man Claire had been contacting via a chatroom. The Angel Collector. Was it the same man who had taken Sophie? And, if so, was the stroke of luck we'd just had a pointer to the future – a lucky omen? I desperately hoped it was.

He poured himself another vodka and sat back in his armchair. The television flickered in front of him, the volume turned way down low. He sipped at the clear alcohol, savouring it as it burned the back of his throat. He knew they were on their way, the screams. They always came late at night when he was sitting on his own, trying hard to hold on to sanity.

The images in his mind were turned way down low too. A necessity. A way to stop them from taking over his life. Not that they hadn't. They *were* his life, those images, as fresh today as they had been when he was a child.

Without warning the sound in his head hit full blast and he was back where he didn't want to be. Five years old, waiting in the dark, shivering in fear and desperate to keep control of his bladder. He could hear her footsteps as she approached his bedroom door and the sweat broke out on his brow.

The door opening, the harsh light blinding him. He felt his eyes being drawn downwards, so that he looked only at her legs, her high-heeled shoes. Her size ten feet. Anywhere but at her face, contorted as it was, in drunkenness and rage.

'I told you to keep them on!' she snapped at him.

He didn't reply. Instead he nearly lost control of his bladder, catching it just in time. A small trickle of urine seeped into his pants.

'*Well!*' she demanded. 'Put them back on! *Now!*'

He whimpered, keeping his eyes down, but it was all in vain. She had no warmth for him. No love, no sympathy. Not until he became what she had always wanted him to be. An angel. Her angel . . .

She strode towards him, pulling him from the bed by his hair. He screamed and screamed but it was no use. There was no one to hear him. No one to help. He was alone. She was the only one. And she hated him . . .

Slowly he did as she asked and began to dress himself again, just as she had done an hour earlier. One by one he put on those hated pieces of clothing, until at last he was standing before her as an angel. All that remained was the wig – long, golden, curling locks. He placed it on his head and felt his bottom lip pucker and shiver. He stood and looked down at his feet.

A calloused forefinger under his chin pulled his face up into the light, into her gaze.

'There, there,' she whispered, the warmth now flooding through her voice. 'Isn't that better . . . ?'

He whimpered again but knew already, young though he was, that it was no use. *He* didn't get any sympathy. The *angel* did . . .

'Little boys,' she began, 'are dirty and smelly and I don't want one. Little girls, however . . .'

She pulled him into her chest, her breasts heavy

against his face, smothering him. Devouring him . . .

'Little girls are like angels. *You* are my angel. My beautiful blonde-haired, blue-eyed angel.'

She hugged him closer still as he felt his bladder give way. Warm liquid trickled at first and then gushed down his legs. He began to sob, repeating himself over and over again.

'It has to stop soon. It has to stop soon . . .'

Waking from his dream, he saw that the television was still on; felt the warm dampness between his legs. He screamed once, then again. His head was ready to explode. He looked at the glass that he held in his hands and threw it against the nearest wall, where it shattered into tiny shards.

Sixteen

We spent the next hour going in and out of Marks and Spencer's in Tooting Broadway. In my head I kept telling myself that there was no point. It wasn't like Claire Burrows's mother would be wearing a sign or anything. MISSING GIRL'S MUM HERE. It was stupid and pointless and the little voice in my head kept on telling me so. There was something else too, a nagging doubt that I couldn't quite work out. Like there was something there that I should have picked up on but hadn't. And all of it was doing my head in.

'Let's just wander around for a bit in case we see someone who might be her,' I said.

'We could just ask for her,' Jenna suggested.

'And say what when they ask why we want to see her? "Er, because we've got a hunch that someone we know might once have possibly seen her daughter at a music festival"? I don't think so . . .'

'Well you come up with a better idea then,' she snapped back. 'We look like shoplifters at the moment – walkin' in and out like lunatics. People are beginning to notice . . .'

She was right too. On our last walk around the store,

two of the assistants gave us funny looks. I wasn't surprised. If I was them I would have given us those looks too. Especially as we had bought at least three lots of sandwiches already, in an attempt not to look suspicious.

'Let's just leave it then,' I told her.

'And go and meet Anna?'

I nodded as we walked out of the store again. 'Once we've been to the shop she used to work at,' I said. 'The one that Jamie told me about . . .'

'Candles and Things?'

'Yeah,' I said, just as someone caught my arm from behind.

'Oi!' I shouted, turning round to see a huge security man behind me.

'Stay there!' he shouted back.

'I ain't done nothing!' I told him; Jenna froze to the spot.

'I've got reason to believe that you and your friend have taken items without paying for them,' he said to me, squeezing my arm.

My head began to swim and little red spots danced in front of my eyes. I was beginning to lose it. Jenna saw the danger and put her hand on my chest.

'Leave it, Jit!' she warned.

'Fuckin' knob!' I shouted, but something told me to calm down. I don't know what it was but I listened to it.

'I'm going to ask you to walk back into the store with me,' the guard said. 'My colleague is already on the phone to the police so I don't want any trouble – awright?'

I looked at Jenna and suddenly I felt like laughing. It was the perfect end to a ridiculous afternoon. But I hadn't stolen anything, and I was pretty sure that Jenna hadn't either, so I told the guard that he didn't need to call the police.

'You can search us all you like,' I told him. 'We ain't nicked shit.'

The guard seemed to calm down when I said that; he let go of my arm, although he was still on alert, waiting to see if I would run. When I calmly walked back into the store, with Jenna right behind me, he looked puzzled and then scratched his head under the cap he was wearing.

He led us to the back of the store, past the checkouts and some nosy shoppers, and into an office, where he asked us to remove our jackets and had a look in Jenna's bag. When he realized he wasn't going to find anything he began to apologize.

'No harm done,' Jenna told him. 'Although you should have had a woman in here to search me. I might sue . . .'

One look at her told me that she was winding him up – and it was working too, until she broke out into a grin.

'I'm ever so sorry,' he said to us. 'It's just that I've been watching you both on CCTV and you've been hangin' around for hours. And then just as I took me eyes off the screen, you headed for the door . . .'

I nodded.

'You gotta see how that might look suspicious,' he continued.

'Yeah – we do,' replied Jenna. 'But we were just looking for someone . . .'

I shot her a glare.

'Someone that works here,' she continued, ignoring me.

'Oh, right,' said the guard. 'And who might that be?'

'I dunno her full name,' Jenna told him. 'She's a manager though. Mrs Burrows . . .'

He looked at Jenna and raised his eyebrows. 'Kathleen?' he asked.

'The one whose daughter is missing,' I added, deciding to take charge of the conversation.

'Yeah – Kathleen Burrows – what about her?'

His tone was guarded and I could tell straight away not only that he knew her but that he was suddenly on the defensive. I looked at Jenna, shook my head at her and then turned back to the guard.

'Look,' I began, 'we ain't here to give her more grief. It's just that our friend is missing too and we think that there's a link between them. We think that Claire – Mrs Burrows's daughter – might have seen our friend at a music festival eight months ago. We're just chasing that up . . .'

The guard took off his cap and looked into my eyes. 'You're not the police,' he said. 'What are you going to do that they can't?'

I shrugged. 'I was just hoping to see Mrs Burrows

and talk to her – that's all,' I replied. 'The police know about the festival and all the rest of it. I'm just following it up . . . as a . . .' Only the words died in my throat. What was I doing anyway? And who was I doing it for?

The guard shook his head. 'You won't be able to talk to her,' he told me.

'Why not?' asked Jenna.

'Because she left is why not,' he replied. 'She tried to come back – lasted about two months but then it all got too much for her. She moved away too – somewhere in Devon. Her brother's, I think . . .'

'Don't suppose you've got a number for her?' I asked, knowing what he would say. He didn't disappoint.

'Even if I did, I wouldn't be givin' it to you,' he told me. 'It was a very sorry time – for all involved – and Kathleen is entitled to have some peace. If you wanna know any more, talk to the coppers.'

'But—' began Jenna, only to be cut off.

'But nothing,' he told her, shaking his head. 'And you could have saved yourselves *and* me a lot of time and trouble if you had just walked in and asked a member of staff. Most of the people working today were good friends of Kathleen's – it was a terrible thing what happened.'

Things just got worse once we got to the shop where Claire Burrows had worked. We walked in and pretended we were browsing through the products. Well, I pretended. Jenna kept letting out a little squeal every time she saw something she liked, which was almost every thirty seconds. Eventually the woman behind the counter came over to us. She was middle-aged and dressed in a long red velvet dress with a purple headscarf covering her hair. Her eyes were made up in green and she reminded me of an art teacher I'd had at school. I smiled at her.

'Is there anything in particular you're looking for?' she asked me, in one of the poshest accents I'd ever heard.

'Erm . . .'

'Do you have any incense?' asked Jenna.

'Yes, my dear – over at the back, to the left . . . Any particular scent?'

'Opium,' replied Jenna. 'My friend had some once and the smell is amazing.'

The woman smiled warmly. 'Yes, it is,' she said. 'And I think we have some in the storeroom. I'll just go and check with my assistant.'

We waited a few minutes while the woman looked and in that time I told Jenna to leave the questions to me.

'Suit yourself,' she told me. 'I'm too busy anyway – this place is mad!'

The woman returned with three tubes of incense and handed them to Jenna. 'There we are, my dear,' she said.

She turned to me. 'Is there anything you'd like, young man?'

I nodded. 'Actually – we're both here for something else,' I admitted.

Her face changed and she frowned slightly, like she was worried. I smiled at her, hoping to put her at ease.

'It's nothing . . . er . . . well, actually it's about some- one who might have worked here once. Someone we met at a music festival about eight months ago. You had a stall . . .'

The woman smiled again, her eyes sparkling. 'Do you know the number of young men who come in here to ask about Claire?' she said, winking at me. 'Such a beautiful creature . . .'

My heart started to pound in my chest. 'That's her!' I said, a bit too quickly. 'Do you know what happened to her?'

She gave me a puzzled look. 'However do you mean?' she asked, obviously confused.

'Claire,' I replied. 'After she went missing . . . ?'

The woman eyes lost their sparkle. 'Missing? But Claire isn't missing at all – she's in the storeroom doing a stock check . . .'

If it had been physically possible to puke with relief, I would have done it right there. Instead I felt my legs go a bit and grabbed onto the nearest shelf.

'What – you mean she's in the *back*?' asked Jenna, her attention finally torn from the candles and things on display.

'Exactly that, my dear. I'll call her for you . . .'

Before we could reply, the woman was gone again. And this time when she returned, behind her was one of the most beautiful women I had ever seen in my entire life. She had soft, auburn hair that fell in natural ringlets to her shoulders. Her eyes were green. And her lips were full and red. She wasn't Claire. At least not Claire Burrows whose picture I had seen on the Net.

'That's not her!' Jenna said in shock.

'Hi,' smiled the other Claire warmly, despite the fact that she must have thought we were nutters.

'Erm . . .'

'What's your surname?' asked Jenna brazenly.

The woman smiled nervously, unsure of what was going on. 'It's Matthews,' she replied. 'Is there something the matter?'

'Were you at a festival last summer?' added Jenna.

'Yeah,' replied Claire Matthews. 'I work all the festivals. Why?'

'Did you ever meet a girl called Sophie Davis?' continued Jenna.

'No . . . not that I can remember . . .' said Claire.

That was when I realized the thing that had been bugging me since the morning. The fact that Jamie had told me that the Claire he'd met worked in a shop. Claire Burrows was still at school when she went missing. She could only have worked in a shop at weekends or in the holidays, but Jamie had made it sound like a full-time job. I just hadn't thought about it clearly enough.

I mumbled apologies very quickly, grabbed Jenna by the hand and dragged her towards the exit.

'I haven't paid for the incense!' she protested.

'Just leave it!' I told her.

She dropped it just as I pulled her out of the door.

I was in shock. There I'd been thinking that I had the breakthrough lead and it had all turned out to be wrong. Claire Burrows *was* missing but she wasn't the Claire at the festival who Jamie had been talking about. Stephen had told me the police had kept the two investigations – Sophie's and Claire Burrows's – separate. Maybe because they had found out that they *weren't* linked. I couldn't believe how stupid I had been – chasing shadows when Sophie was out there, alone and frightened, waiting for me to fulfil my promise to her.

I rang Stephen as soon as we emerged into daylight at King's Cross. He answered on the second ring.

'Jit—'

'Tell me about Claire Burrows again,' I demanded.

'I'm sorry?'

'Claire . . . tell me about her again.'

'Why are you asking me that?' he replied.

'Because we've just been on a fucking wild-goose chase,' I snapped, immediately sorry for it.

'Bad day?'

I paused for a moment, getting my head together. 'You could say that,' I replied eventually.

'What happened?

'We found a Claire at the shop Jamie told us about. Only it wasn't Claire Burrows . . .'

'Oh – and did you try anywhere else?'

'Yeah – the school that Claire Burrows went to. We met some sixth formers who knew her. She's definitely missing but she isn't the Claire from the festival – not the one that Jamie saw. The one he saw is called Claire Matthews.'

'But Claire Matthews might be the one that sent you the text message?' he added.

'No, she can't be. Jenna asked her about the festival and she didn't meet Sophie. Some *other* Claire sent it to me and you seem to think that her surname is Burrows.'

He cleared his throat a little. 'Not me,' he said. 'The police. They told me all about Claire Burrows—'

'Did they tell you about someone nicknamed the Angel Collector too?' I asked.

'Angel Collector?'

'Yes – did they tell you about that?'

'Er . . . no, they didn't. Is this important in terms of finding Sophie?'

I thought about that for a minute. 'I thought it was,' I replied. 'But it's not. I reckon it's just a dead end. Even if the person who took Claire Burrows is the same person that took Sophie – we're still no nearer to finding either of them.'

'I don't know about that,' he said, trying to reassure me. 'Let me talk to the police about this Angel Collector and see what they say.'

'OK – and Stephen . . . ?'

'Yes, Jit?'

'I'm sorry about before . . . for shouting an' that.'

'Don't worry about it,' he told me. 'We're like family – these things happen . . . Just do what you can and try

143

not to worry. We knew it would be a long shot before we started but at least you're trying.'

'Thanks, Stephen . . . It's just that I'm really missing Sophie.'

As soon as the words had left my mouth I regretted them. I felt so ashamed. But Stephen just told me that he was missing her too.

'You know,' he added, before hanging up, 'we're gonna be all right – all of us. No matter what happens.'

Seventeen

Anna was waiting outside the glass entrance to St Pancras when we got there. I was trying not to get annoyed but it wasn't easy, with the crowds of people milling around. In the end Jenna spotted her first.

'There she is,' she told me, lighting up a fag.

'Do you have to smoke that?' I asked.

'Oh shut up, you hypocrite. It's not like you don't smoke too.'

'Not all the time I don't,' I added as Anna walked over to us.

'Hello,' she said with a big smile.

'Hi, Anna,' replied Jenna, smiling back. 'This is Jit.'

'Hey . . .' I said, looking her up and down.

She looked older than us, maybe twenty, and was the same height as Jenna, with curly dark blonde hair and green eyes that seemed warm and genuine: I decided that I liked her straight away. I know you're not supposed to make snap decisions about people but I always did and I liked Anna.

'Sophie told me loads about you – called you a mardy bum – whatever that's supposed to mean in your strange northern dialect.'

I tried to grin but it came out all wrong. I was still thinking about what had happened earlier in the day.

'East Midlands,' I corrected. 'It's not the north—'

'I know,' replied Anna. 'I was just bein' cheeky.'

Jenna smirked. 'Weren't you born in Leicester anyway, Anna?'

I looked at Jenna and raised an eyebrow.

'You've got a good memory,' replied Anna. 'I was born in Wigston or somewhere . . . Little Hill, my dad calls it. Moved here when I was like eight months old.'

I watched a group of youths walk past, all in Burberry caps and Stone Island, holding cans of lager. Footie hooligan chic.

'I see you brought the chavs with you,' laughed Anna.

'They must be comin' home,' I countered.

We stood and talked shit for another ten minutes or so before Anna suggested that we head down Euston Road to a pub she knew.

'It does nice chips,' she told us, 'and I'm starving.'

We'd only been in the pub for about ten minutes when my phone went. It was Stephen again. I apologized to Anna and told her I had to take it.

'It's Sophie's dad,' I explained.

Anna nodded and asked Jenna if she'd had any more piercings since they'd last met. For a moment I thought Jenna was going to get her nipples out there and then but she didn't so I walked out onto Euston Road, into the noise of the traffic.

'Where are you?' Stephen shouted down the phone.

'Still in London!' I shouted back, instantly feeling like a tourist dickhead. 'I'm with Anna.'

I looked around and spotted a little doorway behind me that might cut out some of the excess noise. I stepped into it and turned towards the wall.

'Sorry, Stephen – couldn't hear you – what did you say?'

'I spoke to the police,' he said.

'OK . . . What did they say?'

'Apparently they know all about this Angel Collector. They tried to keep tabs on him on the Internet but it proved to be too difficult. He used too many different sites.'

'Did they say which chatroom he was using?'

'No – he used too many, as I said and, besides, the online name was completely anonymous. There was no way of tracing him just through his moniker.'

'Shit . . .'

I heard Stephen cough violently down the phone line.

'You sound terrible,' I said, not wanting to get into it too much. Not after the last time I had seen him, looking like he'd slept on the streets for a few nights. I knew he was finding things really hard, and to be honest I was starting to feel a bit guilty. Maybe I was making things worse for him and Imogen – raking up feelings and stuff that were best left alone.

'I'm fine,' he told me after the coughing stopped. 'Just under the weather . . .'

Jamie's voice flashed through my mind. 'Australia,' I said, out of nowhere.

'I beg your pardon?' asked Stephen.

'Oh, nothing,' I told him. 'It's just that that guy Jamie told me that six months in the Oz sunshine would see me right.'

'You're not feeling well?'

'No – no, I'm OK. It was just something that . . . anyway . . .' I shut up.

'Well, let me know what happens with this Anna.'

'I will.'

'Can you call me tomorrow?' he asked. 'After three p.m.'

'No problem.'

'It's just that I need to take Imogen to the doctor's.'

I nodded and flipped the phone shut, only realizing my mistake after I'd done it. But then it rang again and I answered without looking.

'Sorry about that, Stephen.'

Only it wasn't Stephen.

'Is that Jit?' asked a male voice with an Australian accent.

'Yeah – who's this?'

'I'm Corey, mate . . . I got a round-robin email about Sophie.'

'Yeah . . . er . . . can you hang on a mo . . . ?' I asked, desperate to get back inside the pub to my notebook. I didn't know who Corey was but he knew me and I had to write down any stuff he told me.

'I gotta be quick, mate. It's not my phone . . .'

I ran into the pub and grabbed my bag. Fumbling out my pad and a pen, the phone still wedged between my shoulder and ear, I started to scribble. Anna and Jenna stared at me.

'Do you know something?' I asked, my stomach beginning to turn over and over.

'Yeah – two things, mate. Firstly I was with Sophie and Ritter just after lunch time on the Saturday—'

'The day she disappeared?'

'Yeah . . . And I know for a fact that when I left them Sophie and Ritter were walking off behind some weird bloke called Shiverin' or some bollocks . . .'

I gulped down air. 'Shining Moon?'

'That's the fella – if you could call him that. Right old—' he began, only I interrupted him.

'What time?' I asked hurriedly.

'Huh?'

'Time?' I repeated, trying not to sound impatient but failing.

'Oh, right, fella. It was close on one thirty. I only remember because I was waiting on a lift and looked at my watch—'

'Were there any other people about?' I asked. 'With Shining Moon?'

'Yeah – couple of freaked-out girlies and an older man – looked a bit *queer*, mate—'

'How'd you mean *freaked out*,' I asked as both Jenna and Anna leaned across me to see what I was writing down.

'Drugs . . . I've seen that before . . .'

149

'And the older bloke?'

'Listen, I gotta go – I'll email you the rest.'

'Just tell me about the fucking bloke!' I shouted, only Corey had cut me off. '*Bollocks!*'

I looked at Anna, looked at Jenna, saw an alcoholic drink sitting on our table, picked it up and downed it in one.

It took me twenty full minutes to calm down and tell the other two about Corey's phone call. As I told them I made more notes on my pad and tried to get things sorted in my head too. He had been with Sophie and Ritter after lunch time, which was just before Sophie's messages to me had begun to get more frantic. He had seen them walk away in the same direction as Shining Moon and his friends – something we already knew about. But he'd also mentioned another man – an older man; someone none of the others had told me about. I wrote '*Older man????*' down on my pad and then shut it.

Turning to Anna, I half smiled.

'You always get that angry that quickly?' she asked.

'Er . . . yeah, sometimes . . .'

'My brother does that,' she told me.

I nodded at her, thinking all the time about what Corey had said. 'So what do you know?' I asked.

Anna shrugged. 'Only what I told the police – if that helps . . .' she answered.

'It all helps,' I told her. 'Or maybe none of it helps.'

'Huh?'

I shrugged too. 'It's like part of me thinks I'm doing this great big wonderful thing – like an adventure story when you're a kid: the kind of thing where you know it can't be real but you still wish it was.'

'I don't understand,' she admitted.

I wasn't surprised. I didn't have a clue what I was on about either.

'What I'm doing,' I said, trying again. 'I don't know who it helps. Me or Sophie's parents or . . .'

'Sophie herself?' Anna added for me.

I nodded. '*If* she's still alive . . .'

'What if she *is* though – and you help to find her? That'd make it all worthwhile, wouldn't it?'

I looked at her and then away again. 'Yeah – and what if she's dead and I just make things worse? Make her mum and dad crazier than they've already become. . . ?'

Only I didn't say that last bit out loud. Instead I asked her to tell me exactly what she could remember about the day Sophie went missing.

Eighteen

Anna went through what she had told the police and what she could remember slowly and clearly. As she talked I divided my list up in my head, between potential suspects and non-suspects. I put all the girls, including Claire Burrows, on the non-suspect side, remembering the brief research I'd done into kidnappings and stuff on the Net. About men being more likely to kill than women. Not that it meant anything – what I'd found out or what I was doing now. It wasn't like I *knew* what I was doing or anything. I was just playing a game . . .

On the suspect side I put Shining Moon at the top and next to him, almost level in importance, I stuck the '*Older man?*' who I'd only just learned about. I also scribbled '*The Angel Collector*' down, although I didn't think it would help. Then there were the two men on my list who I'd learned about from Jenna, as well as from Louisa and Hannah. The first of them was called David.

'He's a climbing instructor,' Anna told me when I asked. 'Although I already told you that. Aren't you listening to me?'

152

'Er . . . yeah. I was just putting what you told me on a list in my head – missed the last bit. Sorry.'

She smiled at me as Jenna went off to get some more drinks. 'That's 'cos you're too clever for your own good,' she told me. 'Write it all down . . .'

I nodded but disagreed. 'I see things differently in my head. It's like I can make more sense of stuff in my head than when I write it down. It's like a written list anyway – it looks the same but it's only in my brain . . .'

'You're just confusing me now,' she joked. 'I like things written down where I can see them.'

I asked her whether she thought David seemed dodgy.

'Apart from his accent? I couldn't understand most of what he said . . .'

I remembered what I'd written down about him before. He was from Newcastle.

'Was it strong – his accent?' I asked.

'*Way aye man* or summat,' she mimicked.

'So what was he like?'

She lit a fag and blew smoke up and away from the table. 'OK – he was friendly, tall and good looking. Had these really great muscles in his back and a load of Celtic tattoos . . .'

I raised an eyebrow. 'He showed you?' I asked, instantly regretting it.

'Er . . . he took his shirt off. Is that OK with you, Dad?' smirked Anna.

I tried to laugh it off but Anna kept on with it.

'I like muscled backs – have you got one?' she asked.

153

'No – now tell me about—'

'Show me . . .'

'Huh?'

'Show me your back . . .' she repeated.

I shook my head as Jenna returned.

'Has he got a nice back?' Anna asked her.

Jenna set the drinks down and then shrugged. 'Suppose so – it's a bit hairy. He's got a hairy arse too!'

I watched them start to giggle at my expense and took a swig of my beer. Instead of joining in the joke though, I used the twenty or thirty seconds to go through my mind-list again. When they were done laughing I asked about the other bloke – Micky, who I had an address for in Edinburgh.

'He was a bit weird,' Anna told me, still trying not to laugh. The corners of her mouth kept quivering as she spoke and then she burst out laughing again as Jenna made monkey noises. And they say that women mature faster than men. I waited some more and then Anna finished what she was saying.

'He knew all the weirdos. You know – Shining Moon and his mates. Only they didn't seem to like him. And then he told us that he was getting out. That they were a dangerous cult. And he had this like mad look in his eyes all the time. Like he was on edge. Told us he was ex-army.'

I nodded and wrote some stuff down. Anna thought it was what she'd just said and smiled.

'I told you it was easier to write it down,' she said.

'It's something else,' I lied. 'From yesterday . . .'

'Cheeky shit.'

'Did you think he was strange – this Micky?'

Anna shook her head as Jenna cut in.

'He was properly out of his head though . . . smokin' bud,' she added.

'Yeah – now you come to mention it,' agreed Anna. 'He *was* all red-eye an' that. That's why we all thought he was just talking shit . . .'

'And now you don't?' I asked.

'I dunno any more,' she admitted. 'I thought they were all play-acting at being some cult, but then the police told me that they really were—'

'*What?*' I asked, a bit too harshly.

'The police – the woman that spoke to me. I called them a pretend-cult and she told me that they were for real.'

'So you think they're the most likely candidates . . . er . . . suspects?' I asked, leading her, because that was what I was beginning to think too. Despite all that I'd learned so far that day. The cult had to be important. I could feel it.

Anna nodded.

'What about you?' I asked Jenna. 'What do you think about Shining Moon and his mates – could they have taken Sophie?'

'I dunno. The police would have spoken to them and they didn't find Sophie, did they?' she pointed out. 'Although you could ring Sophie's dad back and ask him what they *did* find.'

'Nothing – otherwise we'd know, wouldn't we?' I snapped.

'But that doesn't mean they haven't got her,' insisted Anna. 'They could have lied . . . or hidden her . . . or anything.'

'So all we have to do now,' I told them, making it up as I went along, 'is discover where they are based, go up there and sneak around a bit, see if they lied to the police, find Sophie and rescue her. Piece of cake . . . And who knows – we might even get the run-around like we did today.' The sarcasm in my voice was heavy like lead.

'What happened today?' asked Anna.

'I'll tell you later,' I replied, trying not to sound too dismissive. 'Is there anything else that you think could help – anything you know?'

'I think I've got an email address for David. I'm *sure* he said he was moving back to Newcastle for good,' said Anna.

'How does that help us with finding the cult?' I asked, about to be amazed at what she told me in reply.

'David is Shining Moon's brother.'

'*Huh?*'

'Just like I told the coppers,' she said.

The rest of the evening went pear-shaped, as Anna rang in sick to work, and we went and met some of her friends at Clapham Common. To be honest, it was what I needed. A bit of time off to stop thinking about Sophie and everything else. Not that it worked. By the time I was throwing up into the bushes outside Anna's dad's house in Streatham, it was four in the morning and freezing cold. When I was done puking I looked up into the sky and saw that it was dark orange in colour. I looked at Anna and tried to smile.

'She's dead,' I told her drunkenly.

'Ssshh,' Anna replied. 'You need to get some sleep. Come on . . .'

'Dead . . . and it's all my fault . . . I killed her. I sent her away . . .'

'No you didn't,' she told me, trying to calm me down. She failed but a sudden gust of chilly wind didn't.

'I know it. I know it . . .' I repeated, following her inside. I collapsed on a sofa, sobbing silently until darkness closed in and the world went quiet.

She should have been there. Just like every other night. Waiting for him. Only she wasn't and he couldn't understand why. Was she playing a game with him? Trying to hurt him?

A million little thoughts flashed through his head, all of them bad; all of them telling him that she had someone else, which was why she hadn't returned. Where else could she be? It hurt him deep inside, right where he should have been happy. Turning to face the door, he opened the padlock and let it drop to the ground. Pushed forward into the darkness. This time there was no light, no warmth. No love. Just the cold chill of the night, the orange sky outside and the sharp intake of breath from his treasure. His latest treasure. It wasn't supposed to have been this way. Wasn't supposed to have happened so soon. Not with this one. He'd wanted to wait until everything was prepared for the next one. But the next one had let him down.

He edged closer to the chair, the screams in his head stifled by anger and hatred. He didn't want to be this way. *They* made him do it. All of them. Angels that turned into demons and laughed at him . . .

When she saw him her blue eyes darkened with fear. The knowledge that she was facing her final seconds made her whine like a cornered animal. She knew. He knew. All that remained was the act itself. He loosened her gag, listening with barely contained joy as she screamed to the heavens. No one heard her. No one was going to help her. Save her. That was his job . . .

He pulled the long thin knife from his bag and watched as what little light there was glinted off the cold steel blade. He held it above his head as she sobbed and asked him not to do it. Smiled at her fear. And then he pushed it through her neck, front to back, in one fluid, expert movement. Watched her splutter and cough up blood, and eventually die . . .

When it was done and his latest treasure was nestling securely with all the others, he found the mobile and wrote out a message. Looked for the name he wanted, found it and smiled. The point of no return. The beginning of the end. And it felt great. He sent the message . . .

Nineteen

I was sitting at my computer the following afternoon, trying to get over a banging headache, when Corey's email came in. I opened it straight away and sent a quick reply, asking him if he was on MSN. Then I read what he had to say. Most of it was general stuff. How sorry he was that Sophie was missing, followed by a breakdown of all the times he'd seen her or spoken to her at the festival. He had nothing new to add about Shining Moon, just repeating what the others had said: he was odd, with his stupid prophecies and sandals. I found my pad and made a note of Corey's observations anyway and then I got to the really interesting bit.

The older man he'd mentioned on the phone was about six feet tall and thin, but that wasn't the important bit. It was what he'd been wearing when Corey had seen him that made me raise an eyebrow. The older man had been in drag. Dressed as a woman. As I read on, a little box popped up on MSN. I clicked on it and went into my Messenger window. I didn't recognize the sender of the message but I assumed it had to be Corey.

It was. We chatted for about ten minutes, with me

asking him everything I'd asked the others. Most of his replies simply repeated what he'd already told me so I asked him whether the police had been in touch with him. When he said no, I made a note of it and then asked if he was near a phone and what the number was. When he sent me his reply I logged off and used the house phone to dial the number he'd given, with an international code.

'Is that Corey?' I asked when someone replied.

'Yeah, mate – you Jit?'

'Yeah – I wanted to know about the other man. The older one.'

'The drag queen?'

'Yeah – did anyone else see him . . . er, her?'

Corey laughed before replying. 'Yeah – they must have.'

'What about Sophie and Ritter – did they see him?'

'Dunno, mate. They were looking round some stalls and that. Ritter would have mentioned it if he'd seen the bloke. It's not something you don't talk about . . . That nutter saw him though – knew him . . .'

'Shining Moon.'

'Yeah, *that* guy . . . You know you're calling Sweden, right?'

'Kind of. I assumed it was Europe somewhere – it's not a problem,' I told him. Until my dad saw the phone bill that is.

'The older bloke . . . er, bird . . . whatever he was,' continued Corey, 'I saw him give Shining Bollocks some dough, mate. A big wedge of it, all notes.'

'Why?' I asked as a feeling began to grow inside me. Something was about to break.

'Dunno . . . just telling you what I saw. He was askin' him stuff and then they all walked off . . .'

'Together?'

'Well, sort of – Ritter and your friend were behind them. I'm not even sure that they went to the same place or anything. I just saw them go off in the same direction,' he told me.

Something clicked in my head. 'Did either Sophie or Ritter *talk* to the man in drag?' I asked.

'I don't think so, mate. Like I told you – they were standing at some shitty craft stall, looking at the crap they sell . . . and then they walked off in the same direction but they weren't together.'

'OK,' I replied.

I thought for a second about what I already knew. Sophie and Ritter had been with Corey at lunch time on that Saturday. Corey saw the man in drag giving money to Shining Moon. Then Corey left to get his lift and the last he saw, Ritter and Sophie were walking off, with Shining Moon and the transvestite or whatever he was in front of them. I ran through it again for Corey on the phone.

'That's about it, mate.'

'What about Ritter? I've been trying to call him but I can't reach him. Do you know how to get hold of him?' I asked.

'Sorry, mate . . . I ain't got a clue,' he told me.

'If the police need to speak to you – where can they

get you?' I asked, thinking that Corey wouldn't mind. I was wrong.

'Nah, mate. Let's just say that me and the police in your fair country gotta bit of a problem – I only got in touch to help. Sophie was a lovely chick . . .'

'Oh.'

'But I'm not talking to no police. You need any more info, drop me a line. But no coppers . . .'

I told him that I understood. 'What about a man called David – did you meet him?'

'David? Nah – don't know him,' he told me.

'Tall, with tattoos an' that?' I added.

'Nope – although there was this jumpy Scottish bloke . . .'

'Micky?'

'Yeah – that's the fella. Seemed a bit strange . . .'

'In what way?'

'Like I said – strange. He had this look in his eyes . . . like he wanted to kill someone.'

'Did you speak to him?' I asked.

'Only a bit . . . he kept banging on about Shining Moon and his cult. In the end I tried to avoid him. But I'm telling yer, mate – the whole festival was full of nutters . . .'

'What about a young girl called Claire Burrows – blonde-haired?'

'Nope . . . To be honest with yer, mate – I prefer 'em brunette,' he replied.

'OK,' I said, thanking him.

I was glad that he'd given me a new lead to follow

but I didn't feel that he was that important in himself. Everything in my being was telling me that the answer lay with Shining Moon, the cross-dressing older man and the cult. It was time to go and see David in Newcastle and ask him about his brother. The more I thought about it all, the more I found out, the more convinced I was. I didn't know what the answers were or how I would find them. But I felt happier than I had in a long while.

Jenna came round at six that evening, still looking really rough. I let her in and saw by the scowl on her face that she wasn't very happy.

'What?' I asked.

'*You* . . . Why ain't you replied to my messages today?' she snapped, walking into the kitchen and grabbing a chair at the table.

'What messages?'

'Text messages. On your phone?' she said, slowly and annoyingly.

I checked the pockets of my combats but I couldn't find my mobile. 'Shit,' I said, realizing that I hadn't seen it all day.

'You're gonna tell me that you've lost it now, aren't you.' The look on her face was like *Yeah, yeah − tell me another one*.

I shrugged. 'I really haven't seen it,' I insisted.

'So you ain't made no calls on it all day − ringing round all the people Anna told us about? Yeah − I really believe that . . .'

I sat down next to her and put my hands palm-down on the table. 'I've been on MSN and using the landline,' I told her. 'Bollocks . . .'

Jenna shifted in her seat and tugged at her lip ring with her teeth. She was waiting for me to say something. So I did.

'Ring it.'

'What?'

'My phone,' I told her. 'Ring it. If it's in the house we'll hear it, won't we?'

She gave me a dirty look and then grabbed my house phone, daring me with her eyes to say something. I didn't. She pulled out her own phone, scrolled through to my number and then punched it into the keypad before pressing the green button. I waited a few seconds and listened out for my ringtone. I couldn't hear it.

'It might be upstairs,' I said to her. 'Come on.'

Jenna got up and followed me around the house, dialling and redialling my number but it made no difference. My mobile phone wasn't in the house. We gave it about ten more goes though, just to be sure, before Jenna told me to shut up.

'Someone's answered it!' she whispered.

'What?'

'Sssh! Erm, no not you . . .' she said to the person who had answered my phone.

I listened as Jenna tried to work out what was going on. It took all of five seconds for her to start giggling.

'What?' I asked again, not in the mood to play games.

165

'It's Anna,' she said, grinning. 'You left your phone at her dad's.'

'Great!' I said. 'What the hell am I supposed to do now?'

Jenna ignored me and went on talking to Anna, so I left them to it and went up to my bedroom to see if anyone had been in touch. There was an email from Ritter. I opened it and scanned it really quickly, disappointed when I saw that it didn't really tell me anything new. It was just a 'reply to all' message about Sophie and how sorry he was. I reread it just to make sure that there was nothing else hidden in amongst the words and then I signed out.

Jenna was waiting for me in the kitchen, making herself a cup of tea.

'Coffee for me,' I said, half smiling.

'And a mobile phone?'

'What did Anna say about it?'

Jenna grinned at me. 'She's gonna parcel it – next day delivery. Said not to worry about the cost.'

I smiled. 'She's OK, ain't she?'

Jenna nodded and carried on making her tea. As she removed the tea bag her phone beeped twice and told her that she had a text message. She opened it immediately and scanned it. When she was done her face clouded over and she sent a quick reply.

'You all right, Jen?' I asked when I saw the look on her face.

'Yeah,' she said. 'It's nothing – just some idiot sendin' me anonymous text messages.'

* * *

My dad got in at just after nine p.m., about ten minutes after Jenna had left. He eyed me suspiciously when he saw me on the sofa, going through my notepad.

'Where've you been recently?' he asked, sitting down opposite me and producing a banana out of thin air, it seemed.

'Where did that come from?' I said, smiling. 'You like a magician or summat?'

Dad shook his head at me. 'I'm a *money* magician. Keep conjuring up money for you and your mum. Not to mention the tax man, the gas man and every other Tom, Dick or Harry who wants it . . .'

'Get lost, you miserable old man, you're loaded.'

He gave me a glare before biting into the banana. 'You feeling better?' he asked, after swallowing his mouthful.

''Bout what?' I asked.

'Your mum told me, Jit . . .'

I shrugged, not looking up from my notes. 'I'm fine.'

''Cos this pining for Sophie thing isn't going to help. You know that, don't you?'

I looked up this time, glaring back at him, my anger rising. '*What?*'

My dad tried to calm me down but it didn't work.

'What the fuck do you know about anything!' I shouted, storming out of the room. Behind me I could hear my dad getting up to follow. But I was already out of the house and down the drive before he got to the door. He called after me but I ignored him. I walked

167

down to the corner of our road and turned right, bumping straight into some youth on a mountain bike with a hoodie and a cap.

'Move out da way, dickhead!' he spat.

'You what?' I asked, squaring up to him.

The youth spat something out of his mouth and started to step off his bike only I didn't give him the chance. Before he could blink I dropped two punches on his jaw and he hit the ground. I walked on, not knowing where I was headed, and it took twenty minutes for me to calm down to a point where I began to feel ashamed of myself. And then the first of what felt like a million drops of water hit me in the face: the sky had turned red, the leaves darkened and it started to piss down with rain. Something had changed; I could feel it, like the rain that was beating down. Things were getting on top of me and I wasn't sure what I was going to do about it. I found a bench, sat down in the cold and the wet and thought about Sophie.

Twenty

When I got home my dad was still in the living room, watching some news programme. He eyed me as I walked in but didn't say a word. I looked at him for a few seconds and when he didn't respond I went back into the hallway and took off my jacket, which was soaking wet. I chucked it in a corner and went into the kitchen. I'd hardly eaten all day and my stomach was hurting from hunger. I opened the fridge and pulled out some chicken slices and mayonnaise, making myself a quick sandwich. Then I went back into the hall, got my soggy notebook out of my jacket and headed up to my room. It was only when I sat down at my desk that I remembered my sandwich, sitting in the kitchen where I'd left it.

'Shit!'

I ran downstairs, poured myself a glass of juice and grabbed my dinner. Just as I reached the stairs my dad walked out and told me to wait.

'What?' I snapped, thinking that he was going to batter me for swearing at him before.

'Just wanted to talk to you,' he said, quietly and calmly.

'About . . . ?'

'*You*, Jit. And Sophie and all this running around you've been doing lately. You should be concentrating on your schoolwork, not pissing about,' he told me, looking concerned.

'I *am*,' I lied. 'It's just that it's the holidays now and I'm goin' out with my mates.'

My dad sighed. 'In my car?'

'Yeah – if that's a problem though, you can keep it,' I replied, getting moody.

He shook his head. 'I don't want that piece of junk, Jit. I'm just concerned about you.'

'*Dad* . . .'

'Come on – you look like you haven't eaten for days . . .'

I held up my sandwich and showed it to him. 'So what's this?' I asked.

'That's not a proper meal . . . When was the last time you ate with us?'

'I've been busy,' I replied.

'Doing what?'

I looked away. I didn't want him to know what was going on so I didn't say anything. He knew I was upset about Sophie – everyone did – but I couldn't tell him that I was trying to find her.

'Nothin' much,' I said.

He eyed me suspiciously again and then told me that I was strange.

'I'm *your* son,' I mumbled, heading back up to my room.

170

I downed the sandwich in three bites and then picked up my notebook, which I should have left at home when I'd stormed out earlier. It was soggy and some of the pages had stuck together. I cursed myself and then grabbed a new A4 pad, ready to transfer everything I'd written to clean, fresh pages. It took a while but by the time I'd finished I had a few different lists, all neatly spaced, with asterisks by people who I thought were going to be important. And over and over I kept on coming back to Shining Moon, the cult, Scotland and the 'older man'. Following Claire's trail had proved to be a dead end, for now at least. But, from what Corey had told me, it was the other group of people who had been around when Sophie was last seen. And exactly why had a cross-dressing middle-aged man been giving Shining Moon all that money? No – there were too many questions about the cult and the rest for me to ignore.

Five minutes later I'd also made a list of people – male and female – who had seen Sophie at the festival. I looked at it and then wondered whether Anna had seen the man in drag. I called her and she answered on the third ring.

'This your landline?' she asked.

'Well it's not my mobile, is it?' I replied. 'You OK?'

'Yeah . . .'

'I was wondering summat. That guy, Corey, told me about seeing a tranny at the festival – an older man in really bad drag. Did you see him?'

'Him or her?' she joked.

'Whatever . . .'

'Er . . . nope. I would have remembered. Maybe got myself some make-up tips from him. Her.'

I smiled to myself. More and more she was starting to remind me of Sophie and I liked that about her. I decided to ask her again if there had been anybody else at the festival who looked suspicious.

'There were so many people,' she told me, 'there's no way I would remember even half of them. It was well busy.'

That was what I had been afraid of. There must have been so many people who had seen Sophie – there was no way I could speak to them all. Which made me start to question what I was doing all over again. All I had to help me was a list of names, some email contacts and a few phone numbers. One of the people who had been with Sophie last wasn't even on the same side of the planet, never mind in the same country, and I had no idea where the main suspect, from my point of view, was. Just that he was on a farm somewhere in Scotland. Although I did have his brother David's email address.

'You still there, shitty-bum?' asked Anna.

'Yeah – and my arse is clean.'

'And hairy,' she added, giggling.

'Oh don't start with that again,' I moaned.

'Blame Jenna. I mean, it's not like I've even *seen* your arse . . .'

For a second I was about to say 'Would you like to?'

but I thought better of it and instead asked her about David.

'Boring boy,' she replied, putting on a child's voice. 'What about David? He's in Newcastle, like I told you, and I've given you his email address.'

'Any chance you can get a number for him?' I asked.

'Dunno – why don't you try the other girls – Louisa and Hannah – again?'

I asked her to look and see if I had any messages on my phone. She said she needed to use the loo and would call me back later when she had my mobile to hand.

'Make sure you do,' I said, turning to see if I had Jamie's mobile number written down.

I found it and left him a message, asking if he knew David and had a number for him. Then I lay down on my bed and waited for Anna to call back, all the while going through the fresh notes I'd made, hoping to see some kind of pattern or possibility emerge from the page and tell me what to do next; something that struck me as being the clue, the big lead that would take me to Sophie. Anything that would help me to get there, wherever that was.

Jamie rang back twenty minutes later.

'Everything goin' all right, mate?' he asked.

I told him what had happened with Claire. Other than that, I said, things were going well. Then I mentioned the random call from Corey and that he'd offered to help but didn't want the police involved.

'Ah yeah . . . I forgot about Corey. He's not the kind of bloke you wanna mess with,' Jamie told me.

'Why not?' I asked, although I had already assumed Corey was a criminal.

'He's nuts, mate – got into some heavy stuff over here . . . Where was he anyway?'

'Sweden.'

'That'd be right,' replied Jamie. 'His old girlfriend lives over there – Stockholm.'

'Anyway, that's not what I wanted to ask you. Have you got a number for David then?' I said, changing the subject.

'Yeah,' he told me, before reeling off a phone number and email address.

'I've already got his email,' I told him. 'Is the number a current one?'

'I hope so,' Jamie replied, ''cos I only spoke to him yesterday.'

'Why?' said my mouth before I'd had a chance to think.

'To tell him about your problem. I thought you wanted me to ask around?'

'But why didn't you mention him before – when we spoke?' I asked.

''Cos you didn't ask me,' he replied.

He sounded a bit pissed off so I thanked him and told him I'd call him if anything else came up.

'Sure,' he said, not sounding too sincere, but I left it at that.

★ ★ ★

I spent twenty minutes ringing the number that Jamie had given me and getting nowhere. The same thing happened when I tried the number that I had for Ritter's mum in Australia again. Nothing. In the end I left it and sat and watched the phone for another twenty minutes before Anna called back.

'You took your time,' I said, only half joking.

'Jit . . .'

'Did you fall into the toilet or summat?'

'*Jit!*' she shouted at me.

'What?' I asked, getting angry.

'I read the messages . . .'

'So . . . ?'

Anna took a moment before she hit me with a thunderbolt.

'One of the messages – it's from Sophie.'

I dropped the phone and ran for the bathroom, using my hands to hold back the puke.

Year 10

14 January

Jit says:
so . . . . ??????????????????????????

Sophie says:
what?

Jit says:
have you thought about what i said?

Sophie says:
you know i have and the answer is still no.

Jit says:
why?

Sophie says:
because it's the same as before. i've told you this a thousand times. i love you but not like that.

Jit says:
but you love tim fucking shithead that way?

Sophie says:
it's none of your business but he's just a boyfriend. i wish
you'd grow up – sometimes i just feel like

Jit says:
what? tellin me to get lost? go on then.

Sophie says:
jit!

Jit says:
you don't really like me, do you? it's all just a game and that.
you lead me on and then you

Soph01 is busy and may not respond.

Jit says:
typical.

Soph01 has signed out.

Twenty-one

By the following morning I had made up my mind. Everything in my gut was telling me that I needed to go to Scotland and find Shining Moon. All the roads I'd been crawling down seemed to lead to it. Every little bit of information made it clearer and clearer. And then I'd received the message from Sophie. My head was broken, totally in pieces. Like there were ants crawling around in there, taking the different parts of brain in a million and one directions.

I stood and stared at myself in the bathroom mirror. Huge black bags were sitting under my eyes, as though I'd been smashed across the nose with a baseball bat. And that's exactly how it felt. My sinuses were blocked and my breathing was shallow. I hadn't shaved for a week, my head was stubbly and my lips were dry and cracked. But worse than all that were the hollows in my cheeks, which made me look like I was a dead man walking. A zombie. A ghost staring back at itself.

I grabbed the can of shaving gel and squeezed some out into my hand, before spreading it over my stubble, letting the crisp, minty aroma partially clear my nostrils. Then I took a razor and began to remove the hairs, not really taking care at all; cutting myself in several places and watching the blood begin to run down my chin. When I was done I washed my face in cold water, used my clippers to shave my head back down to a number one and then stepped into the shower, which had been on for ten minutes, filling the bathroom with steam – so much steam that as I'd been shaving I'd begun to lose sight of the ghost in the mirror, and had to continually wipe away the condensation with a towel.

Back in my room, I stood at the window and reread Sophie's text from the piece of paper I'd scrawled it down on, wondering what I was going to do with it. The message was short but it told me everything I needed to know. That she was alive. In Scotland. With the cult.

I looked at it again.

I'M ALIVE SCOTLAND. WITH SHNG MOON. HELP ME PLS. I'M SORRY. X

Stephen blinked at me but said nothing. I asked him where Imogen was. He shrugged. Then he let out a soft, low moaning sound and I had the urge to run out of his house. But I didn't. I let him sob and cry, sitting impassively and just watching him. When he was done he got up and walked over to the window.

'What do we do?' I asked him for the fourth time. 'Maybe I should try and call Sophie back. She managed to get the text to me – maybe she's—'

'*No!*' shouted Stephen, making me flinch. Seeing my reaction, he calmed down. 'Sorry.'

'But why can't I call her or at least send her a text?' I asked.

'Because it might fall into the wrong hands,' he explained. 'What if the person who has her hears the phone ringing or sees the text?'

'Oh yeah . . .'

'Exactly, Jit.'

'Or maybe we could check with the police about where the cult is based?' I added.

Stephen shook his head again. 'I don't think they know,' he told me.

'How can they not know?' I asked. 'That's stupid . . .'

'The cult keep moving. The lead detectives update me every so often – I ask them to. And the last time I asked they didn't know where the cult was.'

'But surely if I call them they can ask the Scottish police to help . . . ?' I said.

'They don't know, Jit – trust me. I've asked them a thousand times . . . had all these dreams about rescuing her from them.'

I nodded and thought about calling Sophie again. I told Stephen.

'No!' he reiterated. 'It's too risky.'

I knew he was right but it felt odd not to try and call or text her after all this time. I looked at him and nodded. Something passed across his face, a dark emotion, like a black cloud passing across the moon. More tears ran down his cheeks.

'I knew it,' he told me. 'Knew it . . .'

'I nearly called the police first – that Monroe lady in CID . . .'

I was talking about the officer who had been assigned to Sophie's family after she had gone. A caring and sympathetic woman with warm brown eyes and a beautiful smile. She'd been the one I'd talked to too. I'd almost trusted her.

Stephen nodded.

'Are you gonna speak or just stand there?' I asked him, beginning to get irritated.

'I'm sorry,' he said, lowering his head.

I should have been thinking about his feelings. The shock that he must have been feeling. The combination of joy and relief and sadness that must have been coursing through his heart. But I couldn't and I didn't. I was only thinking about Sophie and the 15.39 train from Leicester to Newcastle, changing at Sheffield. I had to be on that train. I was going to be on that train. I had to find out where the cult was based and David wasn't answering any of my calls. And I couldn't have cared less, right at that moment, about what Stephen was going through. There was a time to be weak and a time to be active. And I was going to be active.

'*Stephen* . . .'

'Yes – I'll call the police and tell them what's come up. But I'm not sure about you going up there on your own . . .'

'You don't want me to go?' I replied, not under-standing.

'It's dangerous, Jit, and you might get into serious trouble,' he told me.

'But, Stephen – we're talking about Sophie. Your daughter!'

'I . . . er . . .'

'You sort things out here – speak to Imogen and let me get on with it. You know I'm making sense.'

Something in his face changed and he relented. 'Yes, OK,' he told me. 'You get up to Newcastle – see this David and then go on to Scotland. I'll sort things out here and then join you. We don't have a moment to lose.'

I nodded.

'And who are you going to take with you?'

I looked out into the garden and studied his perfect lawn. Not because I like grass. Just to have something to look at. Something to calm down my beating heart.

'No one,' I told him. 'Jenna wanted to come but, as you say, it might get dangerous.'

'What about your phone?'

'It's too long to wait for it to arrive. I'll pick up a pay-as-you-go one from town.'

'Well you must text me your number immediately. We have to keep in constant contact,' he told me, going back to sit at the table.

'No problem. I suppose the police here will contact the locals up in Scotland . . .?'

'Yes – I'm sure that's the way it'll work,' he replied.

'Just make sure they don't spook the cult,' I warned. 'Or we might lose Sophie again.'

'I'll make sure they're careful.'

'I dunno,' I said, shrugging. 'Part of me thinks it's best if I just do this on my own. We can't risk them finding out and doing a runner.'

'Like I said – I'll sort that out with them. Now what do you need?'

'Nothing . . .'

Stephen reached across the table, picked up his over-stuffed wallet and started to empty it. There must have been a grand in cash sitting in front of me when he'd finished.

'Take it,' he demanded. 'I don't give a shit what it costs . . .'

I looked into his eyes and saw that they had stopped watering and taken on a steely determination – something that I had never seen in them before. I nearly smiled. This was the Stephen that I wanted on my side.

'OK – we're gonna find her, you know that, don't you?'

'I've always known, Jit.'

He reached across to me and gave me a hug, something else he had never done.

'And when it's all over and she's back here with us I'm going to owe you my life,' he said, 'because that's what my daughter is to me . . .'

I nodded and let him embrace me, fighting back tears of my own. I'd always known that he was a wonderful man and I felt almost elated that I'd managed to help him in his quest to find his daughter. My friend. The love of my life. Sophie.

After we'd worked out the details and Stephen had gone off to call Detective Monroe, I rang Jenna and Anna in turn, keen for them to do a few chores for me; important things that would help me on my way. I spoke to Jenna first, apologized again for not letting her come with me, and told her what I wanted.

'I've got quite a few photos from the festival,' she told me. 'Which ones do you want?'

'All of them, especially any of the cult members or any group shots with people you don't recognize . . . maybe if we get those emailed out to people something might come up – remind someone of something . . .'

'What else?' asked Jenna.

'Stay by your phone. I'm gonna need you.'

'Like I'd do anything else . . .' she told me, sounding slightly pissed off.

'And don't tell no one,' I demanded. 'No one . . .'

'OK . . . *Jit?*'

'Yeah?'

'Be careful. I don't want to lose you too . . .' she said.

'You won't,' I reassured her. 'In fact you'll be getting Sophie back.'

She took a deep breath before replying. 'I know – I still can't get my head around it. After all this time . . . for her to manage to get a message out – it's almost unreal.'

I nodded. 'Something must have happened. She must have got away or managed to get hold of her phone . . .'

'But, Jit—' Jenna began, only I cut her off and said that I had to go.

I was going to end up wishing I hadn't.

Anna sounded excited when I spoke to her and told her to email me pictures of the festival too.

'To your hotmail account?' she asked.

'Yeah, please. And try and get hold of Jamie and anyone else you've got contacts for. Ask them to do the same.'

'Why?'

'Just in case I need to ask people if they recognize anyone.'

'Oh – yeah. That was a dopey question, wasn't it?' she said, laughing.

'You is dopey,' I told her.

'Get stuffed, you northern monkey . . .'

'Cockney cow . . .'

We both laughed for a moment and then I told her I had to go. She asked me what train I was getting and then told me to be careful, before complaining that I would never call her once I'd got Sophie back.

'Of course I will,' I replied. 'You're lovely.'

'But I'm not Sophie . . . ?' she said.

I didn't answer.

That afternoon I got the train with seconds to spare. Stephen had dropped me off, telling me that the police were coming round to his.

'You're a godsend, Jit. I hope you realize that.'

I blushed and told him I'd call when I got to Newcastle.

Stephen shook his head. 'Just text me the new number and I'll call you to let you know what the police are going to do.'

'Oh yeah, right . . .'

'We need to be on the same side, all of us,' he reminded me.

I nodded.

'And, Jit . . . ?'

I smiled. 'Yeah, yeah, I know. Take care . . .'

Stephen nodded, gave me another hug and let me get on the train just as the doors were closing.

It was pretty much empty so I found myself a table seat and sat down, turned on my iPod and settled in for the journey. A release of air and a sliding noise let me know that someone else had entered the carriage. I turned to see who it was.

'Surprise!' said Anna, grinning at me, a backpack slung over her shoulder.

'What the fuck are you doin' here?' I asked, shocked to the core.

'Couldn't resist. Besides, you can't do this on your own – you need my brains. And I brought you your phone,' she said, handing it to me.

'But how the hell did you know which train to be on?'

'Oh come on, Mr Huge IQ – you told me which train you were getting from Leicester, remember? All these trains start in London. All I did was ring up

Midland Mainline in Delhi or wherever and this really nice man who called himself James Brown but sounded like James Patel told me which one would leave Leicester at the time you said . . . Easy.'

I looked at her, thought about it, realized that I was actually really pleased to see her and then smiled.

'God – that took a while,' she said with a grin.

'Sit down, you nutter?' I said as the train suddenly lurched to the right and Anna's head bounced off the window.

'*Owww!*'

Twenty-two

I was looking at the photos of the festival that Anna had brought with her when the train rolled into Newcastle at just before seven in the evening. It was a grey evening with a fine, light drizzle, although we were under cover when we stepped off the train. The first thing I did was light a fag and tell Anna that we needed to try and get hold of David, who hadn't been answering his phone.

'Where we meeting him?' she asked me.

'Er . . . I haven't actually spoken to him yet,' I admitted. 'I was sorta hopin' he'd be willing to meet us if we called him once we were here.'

She gave me a funny look. 'So what happens if he's out or away visiting mates or summat?'

I shrugged. 'Then we're fucked,' I told her. 'Although it's not like I ain't tried to get hold of him. He's not answering.'

'You called Sophie's dad yet?'

I shook my head. I hadn't thought of anything much on the journey apart from seeing Sophie again. I was excited and scared and angry all at the same time. I didn't even have a basic idea of what I was going to do, other than find out where Shining Moon was holed up and go and confront him. Just like I hadn't known what I was doing with the whole 'Claire' thing – I was just making it up as I went along. So much for my stupid IQ, I thought to myself as Anna told me she was going to see if there was anywhere to get a coffee. I nodded and said I would catch her up. I got out my mobile, but before I called Stephen I looked at Sophie's text about five times, just wanting to make sure. Of what, I don't know. She'd sent it from her phone and she was alive. And I was going to find her. Only I should have been feeling more excited than I was. But the only feeling I had was a creeping sense of dread. And I couldn't work out why.

Stephen took his time to answer but when he did he sounded cheery and bright and commented that I seemed to have my mobile back.

'Monroe said it would take a few hours to get things into place, maybe even until tomorrow, but we'll be coming up after that,' he told me.

'You're coming too?' I asked stupidly.

'Try and stop me,' he said, almost giggling because he was that excited.

'Do the police in Scotland know?'

'Yes – and they're already looking into it,' he replied.

'And Imogen . . .?'

Stephen paused for second before replying. 'She's at her sister's,' he admitted. 'We haven't been getting on too well recently but I'm sure things will be much better now – all thanks to you.'

'We haven't found her yet,' I reminded him.

'Ah, but we will, Jit. It's only a matter of time. Anyway, I'm going to drive over to see Imogen at her sister's house and tell her the news. I'll be there by nine. Call me after that if you can.'

I told him I would, rang off and searched my pockets for David's number. This time he answered on the second ring and sounded like he was somewhere noisy. I told him who I was and explained quickly about Sophie and everything else. David told me that he would call me back in five minutes.

'But—' I began to protest, only he cut me off.

I ran up the steps and across the bridge to the main exit. Anna was standing by a coffee bar when I got there.

'Everything OK at Sophie's dad's end?' she asked, handing me a Styrofoam cup.

'Yeah. Come on – let's go and sit down. David finally answered his phone too. He's callin' me back.'

'You spoke to him?'

I nodded. 'Just now.'

We found a bench in the station concourse and sat down, watching people pass by. I'd only ever been to Newcastle a few times before to see relatives and I didn't know where we needed to go or anything. Luckily, that was one thing I *had* planned for. I got out my phone and called another number. My cousin, Parmy, who lived in Gateshead. When he replied I told him that I was at the station with a friend and needed his help. After asking me loads of questions he finally agreed to come and meet us.

'Lucky for you I'm around,' he told me in his thick accent. 'I'm supposed to be working in the chippy . . .'

'You're always around,' I replied. 'And it ain't like you do any work anyway.'

The chip shop was owned and run by his dad, one of my many uncles, and I was relieved that Parmy didn't have to work. Otherwise I'd have had to see my uncle and I didn't want to do that because he'd be straight on the phone to my dad to tell him that I was in Newcastle. And that was grief I didn't need.

'Who was that?' Anna asked me as I slipped my phone into the pocket of my jeans.

'My cousin,' I told her. 'Parmy. He's gonna come up here and meet us.'

'So you do know at least *one* person up here then?' she said, sounding unhappy.

'Yeah. What's up with you anyway?'

She took a swig of coffee and then turned to me. 'You've just spent the last three hours with me and you said like five things – what do you think is up?'

'I was thinkin' about stuff,' I told her.

'I know that but you could have said like maybe ten things?'

'I'm sorry.'

She grinned at me. 'You will be, quiet boy . . .'

I told her to get lost and drank some more of my coffee and then we both sat and waited.

★ ★ ★

David rang ten minutes later, telling me to meet him in some pub, which he said was close by. I told him that I didn't really know Newcastle and that I was waiting for my cousin to pick us up.

'I haven't got long,' he told me. 'Can you be quick?'

'Yeah. Just out of interest though – do you know where your brother is?'

'Yes, I do,' he told me. 'And I know all about Sophie disappearing. I'm the one that called in after she first went missing and told the police to take a look at the nutters my brother is with.'

'I didn't know that . . .' I admitted.

'Just try and get here quickly,' he said sharply, 'otherwise it'll have to wait until tomorrow.'

'Wait for us,' I told him. 'We haven't got until tomorrow.'

Five minutes later my cousin rang to say that he was outside the station and to hurry up. I grabbed my stuff and told Anna we needed to go. Outside there were a few taxis waiting for fares and then, at the end of the line, I saw a silver BMW 3-series. When I looked over the driver flashed his headlights. It was Parmy.

'He's over there,' I said to Anna, nodding in the direction of the BMW.

'Nice car,' she replied as we walked over.

Once we were sitting inside I made the introductions and told Parmy where we needed to go.

'On the Quayside,' he replied.

'If you say so, cos. I ain't got a clue where it is.'

'You could have walked there. It's only a few minutes,' he added.

'Ain't he got a lovely accent?' said Anna, grinning at me.

'Yeah,' I told her absent-mindedly. I didn't want to talk about my cousin's accent. I just wanted to get to the bar and meet David.

'Hold tight then,' Parmy told us. 'I'll have us there in the blink of an eye.'

'Say that again!' teased Anna.

'*Way-hay*, miss . . .'

'Just hurry up,' I snapped, feeling some unknown pressure start to grow in my brain. Something that was telling me to stop and sit down with my notes. Read through them and find a mistake. Only I couldn't stop. We didn't have time. So I ignored my feelings and watched the buildings of central Newcastle flash by.

Five minutes later we were walking past a tapas restaurant and round onto the Quayside. In front of us was a Pitcher and Piano pub and to its right a walk-way down to the river. I looked down along the Quayside and saw that there were loads of people around, all of them out for the night, despite the drizzle and a biting wind.

'The Millennium Bridge is just behind the pub,' Parmy told us. 'We can go over it if you like . . .'

'On a night like tonight?' I replied. 'You mad?'

'Soft southern poof,' said Parmy, winking at Anna.

'Oi! *I'm* a southerner . . .'

'I never woulda guessed,' Parmy told her, his words a blur because of the accent.

'There he is!' shouted Anna.

I looked down to the entrance of the pub and saw who she was pointing at. 'David?' I asked her.

'No – the tooth fairy. Of course I mean David, you dickhead.'

'Well, you know him,' I reminded her. 'Let's go and see what he has to tell us . . .'

Parmy gave me a funny look. 'You want us to wait in the car like?' he asked.

'Whatever,' I replied. 'You can always buy me a drink while you're waiting for us.'

He smiled. 'No worries, you tight bastard.'

Jenna walked through the rain down Queen's Road, past a Citroën garage and an old soda factory, making her way to a small enclosed play area with raised brick flowerbeds, benches and swings. As she entered he saw her and called out her name.

She walked towards him, waving at first, then smiling. Wondering what he was doing there and what he wanted to see her about. It had been a while since she'd seen him and he looked different. Not the calm, confident man she'd first been introduced to. He looked unkempt now. And he was wearing a serious expression on his face. He looked anxious too. She bit her bottom lip, playing with the ring in it, using her tongue. The text he had sent her had been pretty clear. It was information about Sophie, information she wanted to know . . .

However, it didn't take long for her to find out that things weren't right. In fact it took less than a split second. The first punch caught her flush on the jaw, sending shockwaves of pain searing through her head, stunning her into silence and loosening two of the teeth in her lower jaw. The second one landed on her left temple, sending her crashing to the ground. The third one, as she struggled to get up and tried in vain to work out why he was hitting her, knocked the two loose teeth out. Only then did things begin to darken around her.

As she faded she felt herself being picked up like a rag doll. All the while he whispered softly into her ear.

'There, there, my angel – we're together now . . .'

Twenty-three

Stephen rang just as I was following Anna, Parmy and David into a conservatory beside the bar, pint of lager in hand. I put down my drink, dumped my bag and told them I would only be a minute.

'No worries,' David told me, although in his eyes I could see a faint trace of something like anger or resentment.

'Thought you were in a hurry,' I said.

He grinned, but again there was something in his eyes and his grin came over as sardonic. 'That was before I found out that you had Anna in tow,' he replied, winking at her.

I nodded, feeling jealous, and then a fine red mist began to descend in front of my eyes and I started to think stupid thoughts. Who did he think he was, trying it on with my mate? Was he taking the piss, boying me down in front of my cousin? It was only the insistent shrill of my mobile phone that stopped me from exploding into rage. And all for nothing.

Outside the drizzle calmed me down as I listened to what Stephen had to tell me. He'd checked with the police about the cult again. They were asking around about Shining Moon but still didn't have a clue *exactly* where to start looking. I was about to swear when I remembered that I had Shining Moon's brother with me so I had a head start on the police.

'I should find out where they are when I've spoken to David,' I told Stephen.

'Great! Can you let me know asap so that I can tell Detective Monroe?' he asked.

'Yeah . . . Anything else?'

'Photos – you said something about getting some photos together . . .'

'Anna brought hers with her,' I told him.

'Anna?'

'Yeah – the girl from Streatham . . . ?'

'Oh yes – I remember. How come she's with you?'

'Dunno,' I told him. 'She just met me on the train.'

'OK . . .'

'And Jenna too,' I added.

'She's with you?' asked Stephen.

'No – she's getting some photos together.'

'Can she get them over to Monroe?' Stephen asked me. 'As soon as possible?'

'I'll text her when I'm done talkin' with you,' I told him. 'Was Imogen shocked?'

'I'm sorry?'

'Imogen . . . ?'

He waited a moment before replying. 'Oh yes – she's on her way home with me now.'

'That's great,' I replied.

'It is, Jit,' he told me. 'Now go and talk to David and get back to me.'

I rang off and sent Jenna a quick text, repeating Stephen's request, and then I joined the others.

Once David had sat down, the other two left us. I told him some more about what was going on. About the new text from Sophie and the reopening of the investigation by the police. He whistled softly.

'All that from a few emails and phone calls?' he said. 'That's pretty good going for a kid . . .'

I shrugged. I didn't want to smash my pint in his face any more but I didn't like him. He was sitting there all cocky, with his tanned biceps and Celtic tattoos, looking smarmy – like he was better than me because he was in his late twenties. The twat.

'I just did what I did,' I replied, after taking a moment to calm down.

'Still – that was more than the police managed. They must breed you lot clever down in Leicester.'

I shook my head. 'No – they just missed talking to some people. I was lucky . . .'

He nodded, gave me what I felt was a dirty look and then gazed out of the window. I still couldn't work out what was in his eyes but it wasn't friendly.

'So what do you need from me?' he asked, grinning sardonically again.

In my head I told him that I needed him to put his cheesy grin away but out loud I just asked him where his brother was.

'Dunno,' he replied.

'You don't know?'

'Not exactly – I know him and his mates all moved, but not where they are *exactly* . . .'

'Can you find out?' I asked hurriedly.

He nodded at me and then drank his pint down to the bottom. 'Get us another one of these and I'll try,' he said, not looking into my face.

I got up to go to the bar and wondered why he was being so off with me when Anna had told me he was a nice bloke. I asked her when I reached the bar.

'He's been fine with me,' she protested. 'Maybe you just don't like him.'

'I don't,' I replied.

'He's got summat wrong with him,' added Parmy.

'Oh God – not *you* as well,' snapped Anna.

'No – seriously . . . See that tattoo on his arm?' said my cousin.

'The Celtic band thing? A bit clichéd but—' began Anna.

'No, on the other arm – it's an old cross,' said Parmy, cutting her off.

'What about it?'

'I'm sure it's a racist thing.'

'Huh?' Anna and me said together.

'It's a far-right symbol. Not sure what it means but I've seen it before.'

Anna gave me a funny look and then turned to my cousin. 'You think he's a racist 'cos he's got a cross tattooed on his arm?' she asked.

'Dunno – I've just seen that cross thing before and I'm sure it's a—'

'Oh, let's just fucking ask him,' I said. 'I don't care if he's Adolf Hitler's ghost as long as he helps me to find Sophie! Now come on . . .'

'I thought you wanted us to stay out the way,' asked Parmy.

'Come on!' I shouted, turning back towards David, the possible Nazi.

As we sat down again I looked at David's other arm and saw the cross that my cousin had been talking about. I'd seen it too but as far as I was aware it was just the Celtic cross. Then my brain went into overdrive and called up the page of a website I'd once looked at. The cross on David's arm was also called 'Odin's Cross' after the Norse god from mythology, and neo-Nazis and racists wore it. That didn't make the cross itself a racist symbol, nor the person who was wearing it. It just made me realize that David was being fine with Anna yet me and Parmy had picked up a different vibe.

'Nice tattoos,' I said. 'Do they mean anything?'

David gave me a glare and then told me that he was in a hurry. 'I'll call my brother for you but that's it,' he told me. 'And my tattoos are my business, understand?'

'Have I said something to upset you?' I asked, although it was obvious.

He smiled at me, looked at Anna and then drank half his pint down before speaking. 'I'll be back in a minute,' he told us, walking off.

201

Anna waited until he was out of earshot before speaking. 'I can see what you mean now,' she said.

'How?' I asked, not meaning it to come out as snappily as it did.

Anna ignored my tone and told me. 'It's the way he looked at you, Jit . . . Like you were dirty or something.'

'See?' said my cousin. 'I can always tell.'

We didn't say anything else until David came back; then I asked him if he had a problem with Parmy and me. He shrugged.

'They're on a farm near a place called Auchmithie, between Edinburgh and Dundee, close to Arbroath,' he spat out.

'Where exactly?' I asked.

'That's all you're getting from me,' he said, turning to Anna. 'And you . . . you're lucky the girl that's missing is one of us otherwise I'd cut your fucking hair off, you race traitor!'

I stood up as soon as he'd spoken and faced up to him.

'*Sit down!*' he shouted.

I stayed where I was but didn't say anything. Instead I was looking at my pint glass and working out how long it would take me to grab it and shove it into his face if he came for me. I hadn't been expecting David to be aggressive – it was actually a real shock – but that didn't mean that I was putting up with it. Or that I wasn't ready. In the end Anna spoke first.

'I dunno what your beef is,' she said to him, really

calmly, 'but you're a fuckin' nutter and I ain't no part of your race.'

I could see that he was seething and again I was finding it hard to work out what had happened. Why he was willing to help us if he hated us so much. But he didn't explain himself. Instead he just walked out of the bar and left us there.

'What the *hell* was his problem?' asked Anna.

I didn't reply. Instead I wrote down what he'd told us, not sure whether I'd spelled the place name correctly or not.

'Come on,' I said to Parmy. 'We need to get a map.'

As we walked back to his car I thought some more about what had just happened. Was Shining Moon's cult a racist one? To be honest, I was still in shock after David's outburst but I put it to the back of my mind and rang Stephen.

Twenty-four

My cousin let us into the flat above his dad's fish and chip shop, on Sheriff's Highway in Gateshead, telling us to be quiet.

'He'll kill me if he knows I'm here. I'm supposed to be out for the night – which is why I ain't working in the shop.'

'You live here on your own?' asked Anna.

'Mostly . . . I use it as a hang-out for me and me mates. My parents live somewhere else,' he told her.

'It smells,' she added, turning up her nose.

'It's above a chippy, you posh cow. What did you expect?'

I smiled at Anna and took a seat in the living room of the two-bed flat, before trying to work out what to do next. I'd been expecting David to help us, maybe even come along, but things hadn't turned out that way. The only thing left to do was try and call Micky in Edinburgh, the only bloke I hadn't spoken to apart from Ritter. I searched through my notes and found the number for Jamie, hoping that he would answer his phone and talk to me. After our last conversation, when I'd been a bit short with him, that wasn't guaranteed.

But if David had been a complete surprise, with his aggression, Jamie surprised me in a totally different way when I asked him if he had a number for Micky.

'Give me ten minutes, mate, and I'll get back to you,' he said chirpily.

'Cheers.'

'No worries – you get much out of David?' he asked.

I ran through what had happened in Newcastle, just as I had for Stephen after we'd left the bar and gone to a twenty-four-hour garage to get a map. When I was done Jamie whistled.

'I never did think he was right, mate . . .'

'In what way?' I asked.

'There was something funny about them all . . . no non-whites allowed . . .'

I wrote that down in my notes before asking another question.

'So you think there's a racial thing to this cult?'

'I reckon so – especially after what you just told me,' he replied.

We spoke some more and then he said he'd call me back in ten minutes. I snapped my phone shut and looked at the time. Then I remembered Jenna.

'Oh bollocks!'

'What's up now?' asked Anna, returning from the kitchen with two mugs of coffee.

'I forgot to get back to Jenna,' I told her.

'So call her now – knowing her she'll probably be in a bar somewhere with her tongue down some skate-boarder's throat,' she added, grinning.

I dialled Jenna's number but it went straight to the answer service. I left a message telling her to call me as soon as she could. Then I looked around the living room to see if Parmy had a computer. In the far corner, on a small side table, I spotted a laptop.

'Where's my cousin?' I asked Anna.

'In the kitchen – why?'

'I wanna use his laptop,' I replied.

I found Parmy on the phone, trying to calm someone down. It sounded like he was talking to a girl. When he was done I asked him who he'd been talking to.

'My girlfriend,' he replied, looking sullen. 'She ain't happy with me . . . She's in a bar in town with me mates, waiting on us.'

I ignored his troubles and got to the point. 'Can I use your laptop to send some emails and shit?' I asked.

'Yeah . . . but I need to be back in town soon,' he told me, looking even more sullen.

'Won't take long. I don't suppose you've got a scanner?'

'Aye – it's under the table. One of those three-in-one things with the printer and a photocopier. Why?'

I didn't reply and went back into the living room, turning on his laptop and scanner. Anna eyed me suspiciously and asked me what I was doing.

'Just something I should have done earlier. I'm going to scan in some of your photos from the festival and send them out to everyone on an address book that Jenna compiled for me a few days ago. I just think the photos might jog something in someone.'

'Have you sent a reply to the text that Sophie sent you?' she added, completely out of the blue.

'Er . . . I was going to,' I began, 'but Stephen told me it was a bad idea.'

'Why?'

'What if it's taken her that long to find her phone and get a message out, and now she's trapped again?'

'I don't understand,' said Anna.

'Like she only managed to get a message to me in desperation, and if I reply whoever has her captive might find out and get angry,' I explained.

'I get it,' replied Anna. 'We don't want her to get into any more shit than she's already in . . .'

'Exactly. I really think we're close to finding her now. If I reply to her text then maybe her captors will realize that we're on to them. We don't want them to do a runner.'

Anna nodded as she gave me her photos and I began to scan them in. I looked for the ones with the relevant people on them first. All the people I'd spoken to or found out about. Anna watched me and occasionally pointed out some other people who'd been around but whose names I didn't have. She pointed out Ritter at one point and I remembered something that I'd wondered about before.

'What if the police couldn't trace him?' I asked her.

'Who?'

'Ritter,' I replied. 'I mean, they haven't spoken to

Corey, according to what he told me, so what if they never spoke to Ritter either?'

Anna looked puzzled. 'And . . . ?'

'Ritter was the last person Sophie was seen with. They went off after Shining Moon and the older man in drag that Corey told me about . . .'

'What do you mean *after* them?' she asked, excitement building in her eyes.

'Corey told me that Sophie and Ritter walked off in the same direction as the tranny and Shining Moon – they didn't seem to be together but what if they were? What if Ritter was a part of it all?'

'I don't . . .'

'Jamie and Jenna both said that the police seemed to discount Ritter. Isn't that a bit strange considering Corey told me Ritter was the last person he saw with Sophie? Right before she disappeared. Maybe the police weren't even told that by anyone, as they didn't speak to Corey. Maybe Ritter saw the man in drag. Maybe he's the *only* person who can identify him . . . I know for a fact that Jenna and Jamie didn't see him. And Corey won't talk to the police so he's out as a witness.'

'Oh shit,' said Anna, realizing what I was getting at.

'Exactly . . . If the police had been able to get hold of Corey they would have had a whole new layer of clues to follow.'

'The cross-dresser and the cult?'

I nodded. 'The police spoke to the cult but they didn't have a clue about the tranny. It's him!'

Anna looked startled.

'It has to be,' I explained. 'The tranny is the only suspect who hasn't been seen since, apart from Ritter and Corey, and the only one who doesn't make sense . . . Who was he and why was he there? And why was he giving Shining Moon money?'

'But it could be Ritter or Corey just as easily,' Anna said.

I shook my head. 'Definitely not Corey. He was the one who rang with information. Why would he do that if he was guilty? I know he's funny about talkin' to the coppers but he sounded genuine to me. I don't know about Ritter. I've tried calling him but there's never a reply. I'm gonna have to phone Stephen and maybe get him to double-check Ritter with the police. But I'm sure they would have spoken to him – regardless of what Jenna and Jamie said about them not seeming that bothered. They wouldn't have just left him.'

This time Anna told me that she didn't know what the hell I was talking about so I explained some of the things I'd found out since I'd begun my search for Sophie only a few days earlier. I got out all my notes and underlined things for her. When it was all clear she let out a soft sigh.

Just then my mobile chirped. It was Jamie.

'I got Micky's number,' he told me.

I wrote it down quickly before asking Jamie about Ritter again. 'Do you reckon Ritter might just be a nickname?' I said.

'More than likely,' replied Jamie. 'But to be honest I never gave it much thought until now . . .'

'Part of me is thinking that maybe the police didn't get to speak to him and he's possibly our best witness – he's the last person we know Sophie was with. But then I keep thinking that they must have – the police can't have been that crap.'

'Oh, right . . . You don't think he could have taken her, do you?' he asked.

'I've thought about it . . . You saw him after the time when Sophie went missing, didn't you?'

'Because I'll tell yer – even though I don't really know him – he ain't that type. He's just into havin' fun and surfin' . . . I've got a good sense for people, mate, and I left with him after the festival. He didn't seem shady or anything. He didn't take her, Jit.'

'Thanks, Jamie,' I replied, taking a moment to think things through in my head before telling him what I was doing with the emails and the photos. I realized that I trusted Jamie. I didn't even know why I trusted him. It was just a gut instinct based on how helpful he'd been. And it surprised me because I was wary of every other male I'd spoken to about Sophie.

'I need someone to keep an eye on the replies,' I explained. 'And Jenna isn't answering her phone. If I give you my password can you check on my account and let me know if anyone replies?'

'Huh?' he said, sounding almost shocked. Maybe he was surprised at my show of trust too.

'We're close to her now,' I explained. 'If I manage to

track down Shining Moon, things might start happening tonight or tomorrow . . . I trust you and I *need* your help.'

I told him all about the police being informed and how we were so close. And about the text too.

'In that case I'll definitely help,' he told me. 'Can I get you on this number?'

'Yeah – and could you try and call Ritter for me too? Leave a message with his mum or summat? I've been trying to get hold of him since you gave me the number. No one ever answers the phone. I know it's a long shot but can you try? It's important, Jamie.'

'Yeah – no worries. I'll try him as soon as we've finished talking.'

'And you'll help with the other stuff too?' I added.

'Just email me your password, mate.'

I told him I would and rang off. As I watched the photos upload into one file that I could send via email I asked Parmy, who was continually looking at his watch, whether the laptop was Bluetooth-enabled.

'Yeah – why?'

'I've got some other photos of Sophie on my phone and I want to send a couple of them too – family stuff and pics where her hair is different. Just in case her appearance has changed.'

'Whatever, Jit. Just hurry the fuck up or I'm gonna get dumped.'

'One other thing too,' I said as I began to download photos from my phone onto the laptop.

'What?'

'We need to take your car . . .'

Jenna fought back the urge to gag as she felt him get closer to her. She couldn't see him because of the blindfold but she knew he was there. She'd heard him loosen a chain and push back a creaking door. Then there had been his calm, soft footsteps, approaching ever nearer, the soft whistling of some melody that she didn't know. And now, here he was, so close that she could feel his breath on her skin.

'Don't worry about a thing, angel,' he whispered to her. 'We're together now . . .'

She tried to wriggle but her hands and feet were bound far too tightly. Instead she started to sob as reality began to kick in. She didn't know where she was or how long it had taken to get there but she knew it was him. It had always been him. That was when he knelt before her and ran his hands through her hair, across her shoulders and over her breasts . . .

He watched her as she tried to struggle, smiling at her strength. It made him happy that his latest angel was so like the others. Not some shy little girl but a strong-willed woman with fire in her belly. He took out the knife, the blade carefully cleaned and oiled, and looked at it. At her. He knew that things were going to end soon. Welcomed it. The screams in his mind had become too much to bear. It was time to let them go. But not before he'd finished his task. There was a little further to go and he wanted to make sure that he got there. To his final destination.

He reached up and began to loosen the blindfold, excited at the thought of those piercing blue eyes that would soon be staring down at him, filled with fear. And love . . .

As the blindfold came away Jenna saw him in front of her, on his knees. She looked down at the knife in his hands and let out a small whimper before closing her eyes and praying. As the cold steel bit into the skin on her neck she let out a silent scream . . .

Twenty-five

It took about half an hour of arguing and pleading from me to get Parmy to lend me his car. In the end I laid a guilt trip on him about how he had to help me find Sophie. It wasn't a good thing to do but I didn't care. All I was interested in was getting to Sophie – nothing else mattered. Nothing. Parmy agreed grudgingly, telling me to be careful. And then he guided me back into Newcastle so that he could go and see his girlfriend.

'Just bring it back when you're done,' he told me.

'I will,' I replied. 'Thanks for this – it means a lot.'

'Listen – I've helped you out all I can. I'm even letting you take the car but don't think I'm happy about it. Don't take this the wrong way, Jit, but fuck off!' he snapped, before walking off into the drizzle without looking back.

Anna moved into the passenger seat beside me and gave me a funny look. 'You sure know how to get people to like you,' she said.

'I don't care,' I told her. 'Just get that map open and find out how the hell we get to Arbroath from here . . .'

'What you gonna do?' she asked me.

'Have a fag and call Stephen and Micky.'

I stepped out of the car and into the rain; glad of the way it felt on my face and neck. I was really tired and it was keeping me awake. I pulled out my mobile and called Stephen first. He answered immediately.

'Where are you, Jit?' he asked.

'Newcastle – we're just about to set off into Scotland. Where are you?'

Stephen sighed. 'Still at home – the police are coming over in a moment to talk me through what's going on . . .'

'Do they know about me?' I asked.

'Yes and Monroe is none too pleased. She wants you to turn back – let the local force handle it.'

'What about you – you want me to turn back too?'

'No, Jit. What I want is for the police to pull their fingers out and find my daughter. And if they aren't going to then I want you to,' he replied, sounding really angry.

'I can't get hold of Jenna,' I added. 'She was going to email some stuff for me but she isn't answering her phone.'

'What's her number?' he asked me.

I recited it off the top of my head and he told me he'd written it down.

'I'll keep trying her for you. If I have no joy I'll mention it to Monroe when she gets here.'

I yawned and lit up a fag, taking two long drags before I spoke. 'I think I've got it, Stephen,' I admitted.

'The older bloke – the one in drag that Corey told me about – I think it's him.'

'The man who took my daughter?'

'Yes . . . And the guy that I haven't talked to yet – the one in Australia? Ritter he's called. I need to know if the police spoke to him.'

There was a silence and I took another drag.

'Jit – are you still there?'

'Oh yeah . . . sorry,' I said. 'Can you check with Monroe about whether they ever spoke to him? He might have been the last person to see Sophie. I think he might be able to identify the older man in drag that Corey was on about.'

'Are you *sure*?' pressed Stephen.

'*Sort of* – Ritter *might* have seen the man's face: Corey said that Ritter and Sophie walked off behind him and Shining Moon. They went off in the same direction . . . it's a lead, Stephen.'

'But what about this Corey – is he not a witness also?'

'Yeah, he is, but he won't talk to the police. Apparently he's got some problem with them which is why he's gone abroad.'

'And you're sure that you can trust him – or any of the others for that matter?' he added.

'I think so, yeah,' I replied. 'And besides – right now I ain't got a choice . . .'

'I see . . . I'll explain to Monroe as soon as she gets here.'

'Good. I've just got one other person to call –

217

someone called Micky in Edinburgh – and then I'll call back. Maybe speak to Monroe myself . . .'

'That's an excellent idea,' replied Stephen. 'Meanwhile I'll try Jenna's phone for you.'

'Thanks, Stephen.'

'No, Jit. Thank you . . . Ah, that's the door. I'll speak to you later.'

He rang off and my phone started to bleep at me, telling me that my battery was about dead. I flicked my fag end away and got back into the car.

'You know where we're going yet?' I asked Anna as I fished my phone's car charger out of my bag.

'Yeah . . . We need to take the A1 to Edinburgh and then go on from there. That's miles away, Jit – gonna take all night.'

I plugged my phone in and settled back into the seat. 'Good job there's nearly a full tank in this thing then,' I told her. 'Give me the map and try and catch some sleep.'

I checked the route of the A1, realizing that we would have to cross Edinburgh to get up to the east coast around Arbroath. Then I dialled Micky, hoping against hope that he would be in and know where we needed to go exactly. Otherwise, with just David's vague directions, we were lost.

We'd been driving north for nearly two hours when Micky called me back.

'Got your message,' he told me.

'Great – I haven't got time to tell you all the details

but I need to find Shining Moon. Can you help?'

Micky coughed on the other end of the line before speaking. 'They're dangerous.'

'I couldn't care less,' I replied.

'You will. They don't take kindly to strangers and from your name I can tell you're not one of them, as they put it.'

I laughed. 'You mean Aryan?'

'Exactly.'

So there was a racial element to it all. But what did that have to do with them holding Sophie? I went through what I'd learned about the man in drag and my suspicions about him. Micky listened quietly.

'That's why I left,' he said. 'When I met them they seemed like a nice bunch of hippies. All natural materials and living off the earth. But the further I got into it the more I realized something was wrong. They're lunatics. Trying to save the white race from extinction . . .'

'How?' I asked with a rising feeling of dread.

'Selective breeding programmes, isolation from people like you. All kinds of racist stuff with a new-age cloak around it . . .'

'You know, we're nearly in Edinburgh,' I told him.

'Where exactly?'

'Just passed something called Granthouse Junction on the A1. Can you meet us?'

'Keep driving along the A1. In about six miles or something you'll see a sign for Meadowbank Sports Centre. I'll meet you there.'

'Are you sure?' I asked, not wanting to have another experience like the one with David.

'Absolutely,' he replied. 'I'd welcome a chance to get these bastards – it'll be my pleasure.'

I told him that we'd see him soon and put my phone back in the ashtray, where it had been charging up.

'What?' asked Anna, all bleary eyed.

'Ah – Sleeping Beauty awakens,' I replied, grinning. 'That was Micky. He's meeting us up the road.'

'Who he?' she asked wearily.

'The bloke who got out of the cult – lives in Edinburgh . . .'

'Oh yeah – I'm sure he's a nutter too,' she warned, sitting up and rubbing her eyes.

'Ex-nutter,' I told her. 'He wants to help . . .'

'Are we already that close to Edinburgh? I thought it took like two and a half hours?' she asked, looking around.

'It does, only me and my lovely BMW did it a bit quicker.'

Anna shook her head at me, lowered her window and lit a fag.

Micky didn't even wait for me to park the car before he ran out from behind a tree and opened the rear door. It's a good job we were expecting him – it could have felt like a carjacking the way he went about it. He didn't speak until he was safely inside.

'All right?' he asked, in a thick Scottish accent.

'Yeah – I guess you must be Micky,' I replied.

'Aye . . .'

I turned to look at him. He was tall, about six foot three, with long legs in skin-tight black jeans and a hooded top. His eyes were bright blue, his hair blond, and he had about five days worth of stubble on his face. I smiled at him and asked if he knew where we were going.

'Just follow my directions,' he told me. 'The place you want is a small fishing village near Carnoustie.'

'The golf place?' asked Anna.

'How'd you know that?' I asked, amazed.

'My dad loves golf,' she explained.

'Oh,' I said, pulling out of the car park and back onto the A1.

As we drove around the outskirts of Edinburgh I filled Micky in on what had happened and what I thought was going on. He nodded silently as I spoke but didn't say anything. After that I tried to think things through; tried to come up with a plan. But I couldn't. In the end all I had was hope. Hope that I was doing the right thing. That things would work out well. That Sophie would be at the other end of the road we were travelling down. Then Sophie's song started to filter through my mind and I thought about her eyes and her smile and her lips and suddenly I felt the urge to cry.

Year 11

14 October

Jit says:
so whos the new boyfriend then?

Sophie says:
who told you?

Jit says:
not you.

Sophie says:
i was going to but you didn't give me a chance.

Jit says:
rang you last nite. y didn't you answer?

Sophie says:
i was asleep.

Jit says:
at 8.30? you must have been very tired.

Sophie says:
r u angry with me again?

Jit says:
no – just sad. u should have told me. i had to find out from some dickhead at school.

Sophie says:
who?

Jit says:
adam brickhead. he was lovin it.

Sophie says:
it was only one date. he's an idiot anyway.

Jit says:
who – adam?

Sophie says:
no – the guy I went out with. i'm not seein him again.

Jit says:
i dont care one way or another. i told you i'm over that. i just want you to tell me things like before.

Sophie says:
how bout get your arse over here and help me with my work boy?

Jit says:
that'll do! b there in 15.

jitrai01 has signed out.

Year 11

18 October

Sophie's email sent at 22.35 (excerpt):

. . . that it's OK and then you go and get angry again. I can't work you out. And you know what – I don't think I want to any more. If you carry on this way we're gonna lose our friendship and I don't want that. I know how you feel about me – it's not that I don't care but I don't love you like that and I can't lie to you and pretend things are different. I don't want you to feel hurt all the time so maybe it's best if we don't see each other for a while? I know we'll meet at school but I was thinking of outside school. Maybe if you don't come round too often it'll be easier. I don't want to make you feel this way. It's making me feel guilty and I can do without that. We've both got so much work to do and I don't want to mess up my GCSEs because of this. But at the same time I don't want to lose you. You mean so much to me – more than some stupid boyfriend or date could ever mean. Why can't you see that?

Jit's reply sent at 23.49:

I'm sorry.

Twenty-six

'It's definitely them,' Micky told me as we crouched behind a stone wall, soaked to the skin in the freezing cold rain.

In front of us, across a muddy field, was a derelict-looking stone farmhouse, sitting in darkness. From where I was I could make out the doorway, which seemed to be barricaded with wood, and a broken window. There were no lights on at all, either on the ground floor or the floor above. I turned to Micky, wiping rainwater from the back of my neck and shivering slightly.

'How do you know?' I asked him.

He nodded towards a barn to the left of the house as we looked. In front of it were two cars – an old Mondeo and a VW camper van – although it was too dark to see what colour they were.

'The van belongs to Simon,' he told me.

'Simon?' I asked, wondering who he was on about.

'Shining Moon,' he explained.

'Oh, right . . .'

He turned to face me, wiping water from his face. I was trying to ignore the sharp tangy odour of shit that was all around us, wondering what I was crouching in.

'Two problems,' said Micky.

'What?' I asked, stopping my foot from sliding away underneath me by putting my hand to the ground. And instantly wishing that I hadn't, as it came back with some sort of dung on it. I wiped it against the wall as I listened to Micky.

'Firstly we cannae just walk in there,' he told me. 'And second – they are goin' to be expecting us.'

'How?' I asked. 'They haven't got a clue we're coming for them.'

Micky shook his head slowly. 'David . . . the last I knew he was still part of the cult – a recruiter. He might have called his brother.'

I looked at my hand, saw more shit and carried on wiping. 'Why would he help us then? I mean, he was weird and that, but why tell us where his brother is if he's still with them?'

'It's a trap,' suggested Micky.

'So? Let's just go in and give them a kicking. You said yourself they're just a bunch of Nazi hippies.'

Micky sat back against the wall and thought for a moment. Then he turned and looked back over at the house from our hiding place. 'Tell you what,' he said, not looking at me. 'How about I go in and tell them that I want to rejoin the group?'

'Will that work?' I asked, thinking instantly that it sounded like a good idea.

'It will if I take the lassie with me,' he replied.

In another instant his plan stopped sounding so great.

'*No!*' I half shouted.

'I'll look after her – and they'll definitely believe me if I've brought a new recruit. It'd be like a peace offerin' . . .'

I looked back down the narrow lane towards the dirt track where we'd left the BMW, with Anna inside. It was too much of a risk. Too many things might go wrong. At least if something happened to Micky and me she'd be able to get away. I explained my thoughts to Micky.

'Aye – I can understand your thinking,' he replied. 'But she'll be fine – they won't harm her. Remember, if they know you're coming then David will have told them you're a Paki . . .'

I glared at him.

'I'm sorry,' he said, looking apologetic.

I shrugged and said that it was OK. And besides, he was right. Shining Moon, if he was expecting anyone at all, was expecting an Asian person.

'If me and the lassie go in, he'll no' think anything of it . . .'

'Unless he knows that you're coming too,' I pointed out.

'Did ye tell David about calling me?' he asked.

I sat like he was, back against the wall, and thought. It had only been a few hours earlier but my mind was blank. It was too busy thinking in the here and now.

'I don't remember,' I admitted. 'I don't think so . . .'

Micky shrugged. 'Well, we're gonna have tae do summat. We cannae just leave the girl with them.'

I pulled out my mobile phone. 'We'll call the police,' I told him, flipping the phone open and finding that I had no network coverage. 'Fuck!' I whispered.

Micky smiled. 'He'd never pick a place that had mobile-phone coverage,' he told me. 'Besides, they only talk on landlines.'

'They must have been somewhere with a signal,' I countered. 'If they've got Sophie how did she send me that text?'

'Wave it about a bit,' he told me. 'Maybe it's one of those intermittent things.'

I nodded. 'And let's go back to the car now,' I told him. 'We need to come up with something. Fast.'

I used my legs to force myself up and we headed back to the car.

'I dunno why we can't just go in and batter them,' I said as the rain began to get heavier and my legs started to feel numb.

Micky said nothing.

Back in the car I tried my best to stop shivering as tiredness and cold began to take hold. My head was thumping and my eyes were sore.

'You OK?' asked Anna as I checked to see if I could get any reception on my mobile.

'Yeah,' I said, looking at the one bar on my phone's display screen.

'I've come up with a plan,' Micky told her. 'Only Jit here doesn't think it's any good.'

'What's that?' she asked, looking at me.

I shook my head. 'It's too dangerous,' I told her. 'I'm gonna call the police—'

'But we need to make sure that your friend is actually here,' argued Micky. 'For all we know it could just be Shining Moon and a few others. This is one of three places they use . . .'

'Three?' I said, shaking my head. '*What?* So Sophie might be anywhere? Great . . .'

'I don't understand,' said Anna. 'I thought you knew where they were, Micky?'

'I do,' he insisted. 'This place is secret. If they're going to hide anything or anyone it'll be here. There's a cellar underneath the house – a bunker if you like. My guess is that they've got her in there, but we need to go and find out for sure.'

'Nice people,' I heard myself say as I started to get angry. 'How many other people have they kidnapped?'

'That's why I left,' said Micky. 'I've told the police that many times but they never find anything. Shining Moon just brainwashes these kids and—'

I slammed my fist against the steering wheel to shut him up. 'Why the fuck should we trust you?' I asked him, almost in a whisper. 'You could still be with them – just like you said David might be. Tell me why I shouldn't just break your neck right now?'

Micky sat back in his seat and waited a moment before replying. 'Because we wouldn't be sitting here if I was with them. Because I left and because you couldn't break my neck if you tried, you little shit.'

I spun round in my seat and stared at him. 'Come on then! Outside, you Scottish twat!' I spat.

'Oh, for fuck's sake!' Anna shouted. 'Will you two grow up! Just call the police, Jit, and while we're waiting for them we can have a look around.'

I gave Micky a few more minutes with my stare and then backed down. He smiled at me and told Anna that she was right. I looked at my phone again, saw that I still had one bar of reception and dialled Stephen's number. The phone took ages to connect and when it did it went straight to voicemail.

'Shit!'

'What's up now?' asked Micky.

'No answer.'

'From the police? That's a bit—' he began.

'I wasn't calling them,' I told him. 'I was calling Sophie's dad. He's with the police – on his way up here.'

'I see. Well, you can always call the locals too,' he suggested.

'Nah – let's go and check it out first,' I replied, suddenly changing my mind. I don't even know why, other than I was tired, cold and angry.

'But I thought you said—' began Micky.

'Well you thought wrong,' I snapped. 'You comin' or what?'

'Aye, little man – I'm with you,' he said, grinning. 'I owe my friend Simon a little present.'

He said the word 'friend' like it had been mixed with a pile of dog shit and spooned into his mouth.

'What am I gonna do?' asked Anna, looking a little bit scared.

'Stay here,' I told her. 'If we're not back in twenty minutes call the police.'

'Oh great,' she replied. 'It's like some stupid movie. I'll probably get killed out here.' She smiled at me but the look on my face told her that I wasn't in a joking mood. 'I'm sorry,' she told me. 'I know it's not funny . . .'

'Just stay here, babe,' I repeated. 'Tell you what – you keep my phone – if someone replies to my emails, Jamie might call and I have to know what he says. And I need you to try Jenna again – she ain't answerin' her phone.'

Anna pulled out her own mobile. 'You'd better take mine then,' she said. 'That way I can call you if something comes up. Or you can call the police if something goes wrong.'

As she said it my heart started to beat faster. I began to feel less tired and my anger began to rise again. Sophie was so close, so near – I was sure of it . . .

'I'll set it to vibrating alert only,' I told Anna. 'And can you text Jamie *your* number from my phone? Just in case he needs to get in touch with me or something goes wrong.'

'OK. And Jit . . . ?' she said as I put my hand on the door handle.

'What?'

'Be careful . . .'

I nodded and got out of the car into the pouring rain. Micky got out behind me and tapped me on the shoulder. When I turned to him he held out a cosh of some sort.

'It's telescopic,' he told me. 'Snap it open like this . . .' He flicked it towards the ground and it expanded to about thirty centimetres in length.

'Cheers,' I said, taking it from him. 'You got summat too?'

Micky grinned at me. 'Aye, wee man, that I have,' he told me before setting off down the dirt path and into a muddy field, towards the farmhouse.

The harsh light from the lamp he'd switched on woke Jenna up. At first her eyes flinched from the artificial daylight but within a few moments they adjusted and she looked at her surroundings. She was in a room of some sort, like a bedroom, but with grey concrete walls and ceiling, and no window. He'd placed her on a bed, with proper covers that smelled even worse than the rest of the room. Dried sweat and other things she didn't want to think about. Her hands and feet were still tied, restricting the amount she could see, but what she could make out seemed familiar.

The cut on her neck stung where he had applied neat TCP but she welcomed the pain. That moment, whenever it had been, when he'd raised the blade to her neck, it had felt like it would be her last. But here she was, alive and thankful for that small mercy.

The groaning began moments later. A muffled noise, like someone trying to speak from behind a gag. It was coming from behind her. She tried to turn but couldn't. Instead she turned her head as far back as she could but still she couldn't see who was moaning. She returned to her original position and thought for a moment. Beneath her the springs in the mattress creaked and moved. She swung herself hard to the left, trying to gain momentum. She did it again, and again. On the fifth go she felt herself turning, felt the ties round her hands and feet tighten and cut into the flesh. But she ignored the pain, desperate to see more of the room. To find out who was behind her.

She rolled right off the edge of the single bed and hit the ground face down. A sharp pain shot through her shoulders and the air was forced out of her lungs. She lay where she was for a short while, trying to catch her breath. When she had she turned her head and looked up into bright blue eyes that she recognized almost instantly. The owner of the bright blue eyes returned that recognition and moaned even louder. As Jenna began to scream, the few remaining contents of her stomach began to work their way up into her throat . . .

He turned up within seconds, looked down at her and sneered.

'Should have stayed where you were,' he whispered. 'Now I'm going to have to hurt you and I didn't want to do that.'

She looked up at him, pleading with her eyes as the full horror of what was happening filled her with dread. It didn't last long though. The final thing she saw before darkness was his right foot, heading straight for her face . . .

Twenty-seven

Micky raised his left forefinger to his lips and gestured towards a partially boarded window.

'In there,' he whispered.

I nodded at him as he moved his head closer to me.

'I'll go in first,' he continued. 'Make sure it's safe. Then you follow.'

He turned to the window and, using the light from his mobile phone's display, leaned in and tried to see what was inside. Then he used the ledge to lift himself up and swung his legs through the gap, all in one movement. After a few seconds he stuck his head out and nodded at me, and I followed him into the farmhouse, trying not to make too much noise.

Inside the air was damp and smelled of grit and dirt and faeces. As I followed the light from Micky's mobile I fought back the urge to retch. He moved quickly through the room as though he knew exactly where he was going and for a moment I panicked and thought that he was taking me into a trap. After all, I didn't know him. It was crazy to be so trusting of him. I looked down at the cosh in my hands and thought about using it on the back of his head. But just as suddenly as it had arrived the feeling of paranoia disappeared. I breathed a sigh of relief.

I followed him into the next room, catching my thigh on a nail, ripping my jeans. 'Shit!'

'Shut it!' he whispered, stopping abruptly.

'Where are we going?' I asked in a low voice.

'Just checking out the house,' he told me. 'But my guess is that they're either in the cellar or the barn.'

I nodded as Micky walked on, into yet another room. But at the entrance to this one he stopped and held me back.

'What?' I asked, after bumping into him.

'Stay still and shut up!' he demanded in a menacing whisper.

As I fought back yet another urge to smack him in the head he lifted his mobile into the air and let the light from the display illuminate part of the room. From what I could make out it had once been a kitchen. On the back wall, furthest away from us, was a sink, hanging loose from the wall. Above it was a window and, to the left, a door. The door was slightly ajar. But then the display light faded. Micky pressed a button and it came on again.

The door seemed to be swaying slightly and this time I also made out what looked like steel traps spread across the floor in front of us. Micky crouched down and had a closer look.

'Ankle breakers,' he told me.

'So they do know we're coming,' I whispered.

Micky shook his head. 'They might be here just as a

safeguard,' he told me. 'Just in case *anyone* turns up . . .'

My stomach turned over as I thought about why they would need so desperately to keep people out. There could have been a few reasons but none of them were good.

'Let's get out of here and call the police,' I suggested, only for Micky to shake his head.

'Just follow me. *Carefully*. Put your feet down directly in the space mine leave. Come on!'

I watched as he moved slowly and deliberately through the kitchen, keeping the light directed at the floor. And I did as he'd asked, being very careful to follow his steps exactly. It worked for the first couple of metres but then I felt myself swaying and nearly fell into the traps. Micky caught me at the last moment and pulled me upright.

'Thanks,' I said, full of relief.

'Ye're welcome,' he told me, grinning like a madman.

'What's so funny?' I asked, lowering my voice.

'This,' he replied, lowering his voice too. 'I'm longing to get these bastards. It feels great . . .'

'This ain't about you,' I reminded him in a whisper.

He looked at me for a moment and then grinned again. 'For you it's about Sophie,' he whispered back. 'For me – it's about so many other things too.'

I wanted to ask him what he was talking about but I didn't. Besides, I could work it out for myself. Something about his time with the cult had planted a seed in his head. Vengeance. And as long as he was on my side I was happy with that. Instead, as we made it to the door without losing a foot, I asked him something else that had been on my mind.

'You were in the army, weren't you?' I said.

Micky ignored me and opened the door slowly, backing into me as he did. Then he edged through, pulling me along by my top. Through the door was a sort of gazebo area – open on all sides except the top, where sheets of corrugated metal formed a roof.

'Yes – I was in Three Para,' he said finally. 'Can ye tell?'

I nodded.

We moved into the covered area slowly, careful not to make too much noise, although my brain kept telling me that it didn't matter anyway. They knew we were coming. I could feel it in my gut.

Beyond the covered area the rain had begun to hammer down more forcefully than ever and a strong wind picked up. Out of the corner of my eye I saw something move along the floor. I jolted.

''S only a rat,' Micky told me. 'Big bugger too – make a great supper.'

'Nice,' I replied.

He pointed out into the yard, beyond the cover of the roof. I tried to make out what he was pointing to but the light just wasn't good enough.

'Trapdoor,' he told me. 'Leads down into the bunker.'

'You think it might be booby trapped or something?' I asked.

'Probably,' he replied, moving towards it.

Suddenly the wind howled and in the middle distance I heard a tree crash to the ground and the sound of splintering wood.

'Come on!' he insisted.

As soon as we left the cover the rain began to sting my face, running down my neck and back, making me shiver. I looked left and right, hoping to see what was coming, if there was anything, but it was too dark. I could barely make out Micky, who had moved about five metres ahead of me. He was just a black mass and I followed that. Eventually both of us were standing by the trapdoor, which seemed to be covered in grass. But as I knelt down in the mud, I could see the edges of it. Micky knelt beside me.

'What now?' I asked, but then Anna's mobile began to vibrate against my leg. 'Hang on.'

I pulled the phone out of my pocket and answered it. It was Anna.

'Jamie just called,' she told me. 'Are you OK?'

'Yeah,' I whispered. 'What did he say?'

'You've had an email from Ritter.'

'And . . . ?'

'And that's all he said. Ritter is gonna email again when he's had a chance to look at the pictures you sent – plus I gave him the number for my phone too. Just in case.'

I shook my head. 'Why didn't he just look at the pictures and then email me?'

'I dunno, Jit. I'm just passing on a message, OK?'

'Sorry,' I said, realizing that I had snapped at her. 'You get in touch with Jenna?'

'No – she ain't answering her phone. I'll keep tryin' though. You still want me to call the police? Only you've already been gone twenty minutes.'

I thought about it for a second. 'No,' I replied. 'Give us a bit more time. Another fifteen minutes.'

'OK – one other thing . . .' she added.

'What's that, babe?'

'Sophie's dad rang. He seemed a bit odd . . .'

'Is he on his way with the police?' I asked.

'Yeah, but he sounded like he was sobbing or summat.'

'Don't worry about that,' I told her. 'He's having a rough time. Did he say how long they would be?'

'No,' said Anna. 'Just that it would be soon.'

'OK,' I said. 'Look, I better go. Keep in touch.'

'OK,' she replied.

I put the phone away and looked around. Micky was gone. I peered behind me and over to the left but there was no sign of him. Telling myself not to panic, I stayed where I was, feeling around the trapdoor for a finger hold. When I found it I tried to lift it but it held firm.

'Shit!' I whispered to myself before looking for Micky again.

In my head I told myself that he must have gone off for a good reason and that if he'd wanted me to move he would have told me. So I sat still and let the rain soak me down to the bone as sheet lightning began to crack and fizzle across the sky, lighting things up for a split second at a time. I felt the muzzle in the back of my head after the third flash in quick succession.

'Don't move, you bastard!'

Like a dickhead I tried to turn round but I didn't get far. Instead I ended up face down in the mud with a foot in my back. I gasped, taking in mud, and began to cough and choke as the foot pushed down harder. Only when I thought that my head was about to explode did the pressure stop. I rolled over, spitting out mud and shit and trying to take in air. My eyes were covered in muck too but I could just about make out someone standing over me. I recognized him from the festival photos. It was Shining Moon, pointing a rifle at my face.

'Hello,' he said, smiling like a maniac.

Twenty-eight

As Shining Moon led me towards the barn, my hands laced behind my head, he told me to call him Simon.

'It's not as though we don't know each other,' he told me, stabbing the back of my head with the rifle.

'Where's Sophie?' I replied through gritted teeth as I fought back the urge to do something really stupid and tackle a man with a gun.

'After all,' continued Simon, completely ignoring what I'd just said, 'you've been asking about me all over the place. Well here I am . . . *Happy?*'

I closed my eyes for a second and different faces flashed in front of my eyes: Sophie, Anna, Jenna, my parents, Stephen, Imogen. People I might never see again. I shook my head, trying to stop the negative thoughts that were forming, like cancerous tentacles, in my mind. I had to keep a clear head. Had to think. Think . . .

The barn door creaked and groaned as Simon pulled it open, just enough to let us both in. I led the way, blinking like a nutcase, trying to see what was happening, to make out shapes in the darkness.

'Keep walking in a straight line,' he ordered.

I stumbled forward, catching my shin against some-thing wooden, but managing not to fall. About ten steps further on I walked into a post.

'Stop.'

I stood still, flexing the muscles in my arms behind my head to keep them loose. I heard and felt one of my knuckles crack.

'That'll give you arthritis,' he told me. 'Bad for your health. But then so is messing with me . . .'

I heard him pull out something metallic and very quickly he was cuffing me to the post with his free hand. I didn't even have time to react before I was standing facing him, with my arms tight behind my back.

'There – that's better,' he said, getting right up in my face.

I looked at his nose as he sneered at me, his face so similar to his brother David's that they might have been twins. Only Simon's hair was long and greasy, not military-style short. My eyes left his nose momentarily. I was weighing up my options. One lunge and I'd have his nose between my teeth. But then reason caught up with me. Even if I did hurt him it wasn't going to help me out of the cuffs, wasn't going to help me find Sophie. And it wasn't going to save my life. So I let it go, concentrating instead on being ready for the next chance I got . . .

'And your friend in the car,' he told me, sending a chill down my spine. 'Some of my brothers and sisters will see to her . . .'

I struggled against the pole, the handcuffs digging into the skin of my wrists. Not that it was any use. I was at his mercy.

'You touch her,' I told him, 'and I'll cut your hair off and feed it to you.'

'Is that *all*?' he asked, smiling. 'And there was me thinking that you dark ones were imaginative when it comes to punishment . . .'

'Dark ones?'

'You and your kind,' he spat out. 'Growing inside the womb of Albion, eating at the mother's flesh . . . like the virus that you are . . .'

For a moment he threw me with Albion but then my memory dug up another useless fact that I'd picked up somewhere. Albion was an ancient term for Great Britain, mostly used by writers and poets. I was dealing with a literary racist. I smiled at him, figuring out that it would be the most annoying thing I could do. It might anger him, and anger might lead to mistakes. It didn't work.

'Oh, you think it's funny, you vampire? That your filthy kind are drinking our beloved lands dry and tainting our purest souls with perversion and sin? Well, smile all you like because very soon my brothers and sisters will rise up and take back what belongs to us. To me . . .'

He let the last two words hang in the air, maybe hoping for a reaction, but I kept quiet, wondering instead exactly *how* insane he was. He lost interest then, propping the gun up against a bale of straw and pushing what looked like a rotten cart to one side. Then he fell to his knees and started to move straw and sawdust into a heap. Eventually he pulled at something and the floor came up in one creaking movement. It was a trapdoor. Another one.

'Seems as though our traitorous brother Micky didn't know about this entrance,' he told me, standing up and grabbing the rifle.

'Where is he?' I asked.

'With Brother David – making recompense for his betrayal . . .'

Another chill worked its way down my back as I realized that we had indeed walked right into a trap.

'I don't get it,' I told him. 'David called the police about Sophie . . . gave you up.'

'Ah, and there I was thinking you were a particularly clever one. The police reacted to the bone we threw them like the dogs that they are. Perhaps with different masters they'd have learned the art of bluffing.'

'What – so you arranged for David to betray you as a *bluff*?'

I worked through it in my head. What was the point of drawing attention to themselves over the case of a missing girl? What good could it possibly have done? When the answer came to me it made complete sense.

'The police see that you ain't got her and that puts you in the clear,' I said. 'No longer the suspects.'

Simon nodded. 'No missing girl, no evidence, no games. Just a polite welcome, a cup or two of nettle tea and complete co-operation. Those dogs left with smiles on their faces.'

'And what happened to Sophie?' I added, hoping to catch him on the hop.

He shrugged. 'She went away for some special enlightenment – similar to what Brother Micky is going through right now. Minus *some* of the pain, perhaps . . .'

As if his words had been some kind of sign, a scream rang through the night air. A man's voice.

'Not that we had her for very long, mind you. She was a *special* case. Now if you'd just allow me to escort you down into the bunker . . .' Simon said, walking behind me and undoing the handcuffs slowly.

My head began to swim. What if Sophie wasn't with them? If we had just walked into a trap for nothing then how the hell was I going to find Sophie now? Once again I had no chance to react as Simon removed the cuffs before the rifle was at my head again.

'Walk slowly down the stairs,' he told me. 'And don't get any ideas. There are others waiting for us – and not all of them are as amiable as I am.'

I felt the anger begin to rise again, this time tinged with fear. The fear was making me sweat like you would on a hot, humid summer's night in August. I could feel my T-shirt clinging to my back and beads of perspiration gathering at my hairline. But I knew my anger was useless and that in turn made me even angrier – and reckless too. I decided to push him.

'Why Shining Moon?' I asked as I moved towards the secret entrance. 'I mean, you sound like you should be a gay lapdancer or summat.'

'Ah – humour. I like it,' he replied, not falling for the bait.

'But it is a stupid name,' I continued.

'Only to you,' he said as I started down the steps into the semi-darkness, aware that there was a light on somewhere below.

'Oh come on – you must have spent all of three seconds thinking it up.'

He stabbed the rifle into my head three times before replying. 'OK,' he said. 'Seeing as you're about to leave this mortal coil anyway. My people are living in a perpetual darkness because of you and your virus—'

'What *virus*, you dickhead?' I interrupted, hoping that I'd got to him. Hoping for a mistake . . .

'The dark ones – a human virus spreading un-controlled across the planet. Leaving the pure white race in total darkness – no light, no hope. Well, I'm changing all that. I'm a beacon in the night sky, a ray of light in the darkness. A shining light – the shining moon . . .'

I started laughing. I don't even know why. It was just so fucking stupid, what he was telling me. But it didn't get to him enough. He didn't make a mistake. Instead I felt his foot in my back and I made the rest of my journey down into the bunker in a headlong freefall, hitting the floor with a jolt.

'Laugh at that,' Simon sneered from above me.

★ ★ ★

Micky was tied to a chair when I limped into the bunker, his eyes never catching mine. I looked at his face, battered and broken, at the swelling round his eyes and the knotted bruise sitting on the left of his forehead, high up in his hairline, like half an egg. And then when David pulled another chair alongside him and tied me to it I saw the bloody mess that was the left side of his head, hastily bandaged. I looked around in terror; saw only smiles and hatred from the other faces there. Two more men and three women, standing around the edge of the room, watching our every move, silent as ghosts. And then I looked down into Micky's lap and saw his left ear, cleanly severed and lying on a blood-soaked tissue. The second scream that I heard that night was mine . . .

Twenty-nine

After the second call Anna put the mobile down on the seat next to her. She looked at her watch again. Jit and Micky had been gone for over half an hour. She picked up the phone again, looked at it and wondered whether she should call the police. But she didn't call. Instead she pocketed the phone, opened the car door and stepped out into the rain and the darkness.

The lane they had parked on was covered by overhanging branches, so much so that it looked like a tunnel. She walked towards the small gap that Jit and Micky had taken, into a muddy field. Looking across the field, she could just about make out the shapes of the house and barn. She pulled the phone from her pocket to see if it had any signal. There was one bar showing, weak but maybe enough to get through to the police. She waited a moment and then dialled, putting the phone to her ear. Just as the dialling tone set in she heard a noise from the track and then a voice, swearing. She jumped and turned round, heading for the gap in the tree line. Hoping that it would be Jit and Micky, she peered through.

She heard the voices of two men and then a woman and then saw torch beams lighting up the track. Were they members of the cult? If they were by the car it could only mean one thing. They knew she was there and Jit and Micky were in trouble.

Quickly, and as quietly as she could, she moved into the field, knowing that she had to get away from them. They had obviously been sent to get her. She felt herself slip and slide on the slick, muddy ground, thankful that she had chosen to put her trainers on when she'd left home. Suddenly home seemed a long way away; she felt she'd been away for days. She moved towards the centre of the field, looking at the phone again. The one bar of reception was gone. She whispered a curse and then moved on, hoping to find a spot from which to call the police.

Halfway across the field she heard them behind her. They were shouting to each other. She turned her head but continued walking. They had torches and were shining them towards her. She turned to face the way she was going, looked at the phone, saw two bars and stopped. She dialled the police again and waited for a reply. It came on the third ring. After all the preliminaries about what service she wanted she was put through to a switchboard operator.

'I need help!' she whispered.

'I need a name and an address, miss,' came the reply.

'There are people chasing me through a field,' she replied, getting angry. 'They've got my friends . . . it's some kind of cult. I'm near a place called—'

'Just stay calm,' ordered the woman on the other end of the phone. 'Can you tell me exactly where you are?'

'In a field . . . somewhere near the east coast of Scotland, near Arbroath. It's by Carnoustie. A small fishing village near there – help!'

Anna turned to see that her pursuers were getting closer. Her brain went into overdrive.

'There's a farmhouse down a lane, about two miles up the road from the village. It's called Auch . . . something . . . they've got my friends . . .'

'Who has your friends, miss?'

'Shining Moon!' shouted Anna, realizing that she had to run.

Remembering something that she'd seen on a TV cop show, she tossed the phone to the ground, leaving the channel open and connected, hoping that they would be able to find the place. Then she turned and ran for her life . . .

He was standing with his back to Jenna when she opened her eyes, half naked, wearing only women's lingerie and a pair of royal-blue socks. She winced at the sight, her stomach turning, and only when she'd fought back the urge to retch did she look around and see that she'd been moved. She was still tied up, this time to a chair, but her head was moving more freely now. The pain stabbed into her shoulder, making her wince as she studied her environment. The room they were in now was darker and smaller than the one before. And this time there were only the two of them.

He seemed to be standing in front of a yellowing, rusty chest freezer, the lid open. He was holding something. She tried to get a look but his body blocked her view. Instead she turned away and had another look at her surroundings as a terrible, acrid smell began to rise in her nostrils. As she fought back vomit a second time he turned to her and smiled. In his hands was a severed head.

Jenna let herself puke over and over again, forcing her head to one side, away from him and what he held. Her mind began to race, a kaleidoscope of different fears rolling into one big horrific realization, and she started to sob. He was going to kill her, she knew it. And even though she tried not to look at the greying and wrinkled head in his hands, something drew her eyes to it.

There was very little hair left and the skin, where it remained, was withered and shrunken. The eye-sockets held nothing save a few scraps of what also looked like shrivelled skin. But the lower part of the face seemed almost normal. She looked away and then back again, trying to work out why the area around the mouth seemed so strange. That was when she realized that he had applied lipstick to what was left of the lips . . .

He edged forward, moving slowly and deliberately. The hideous thing in his hands seemed to grin at her. Jenna tried to push herself up, arching her back, trying to get away, but it was no use. He came to a stop less than thirty centimetres from her. The only thing separating her face from his groin was the head. She looked at him, imploring him with her eyes, but it was no use.

'Here,' he said to her as she lost control of her bladder. 'Meet one of my angels – unfortunately I had a moment of madness with this one. Had to redesign her face a little. A little kiss, perhaps . . .'

She arched backwards yet again, feeling the chair rock beneath her, as he pushed the severed head forward, pressing its mouth against hers . . .

Thirty

Two men followed the short, stocky woman into the bunker. All three of them looked sullen. The woman whispered something to Simon. His face flushed red as he looked over at me. The newcomers seemed to turn themselves off then – they stood quietly where they were, almost fading into the background – as nameless and faceless as the other cult members. Like sheep cowed by a shepherd and his dog. Or shop-window dummies acting as silent witnesses. I wondered if they were on drugs or something.

'Seems as though your little friend has run away,' Simon told me.

'Fuck off,' I replied – it was all I could think of saying. I was relieved that Anna had escaped them. Then I asked him where Sophie was.

Simon ignored me, turned and went across to another doorway, this one shut. He banged a balled fist against the wooden door. It opened after a few seconds. I looked past Simon and saw David, his brother, and, beyond him, some kind of small, office-type space. The light of an LCD display flickered, telling me that he had a PC in there. I strained to see what else I could make out but David saw me and stepped into the bunker, shutting the door behind him.

Next to me I heard Micky's chair creak slightly. I turned towards him slowly, careful not to look down at the severed ear in his lap. His eyes were open and one of them was blinking madly. I was about to ask him if he was OK when I realized that it would have been the stupidest question I had ever asked anyone. But then he stopped blinking and turned his head my way, his eyes trying to tell me something. I searched them for some kind of clue but it was no use. And he couldn't tell me out loud, partly because they would hear him and partly because his mouth was so swollen from the beating he'd taken.

I looked back at Simon and his brother, still aware of the other cult members, but only because they were so quiet and disengaged.

'You ain't gonna find Anna,' I told them. 'I know she's already called the police—'

'Shut up!' shouted David.

'Too clever for you,' I replied. 'She was at that festival too – the one where you took Sophie and she didn't fall for your shit—'

'I said *shut up!*' he repeated, his face going red.

'Where's Sophie?' I demanded again.

David looked at his brother and then smiled at me. 'Far away from you,' he told me. 'So you can't pollute her—'

'Where *is* she, you stupid wannabe Nazi?'

Simon held a hand out in front of his brother, as if to

255

hold him back. Only David hadn't made any kind of move towards me.

'What are you?' I asked Simon. 'The Messiah *and* psychic? Must be busy in your head, you stupid, pompous twat.'

'Just shut up, will you?' he replied, trying to sound nonchalant. 'It's hard keeping David on a leash at the best of times. Just look at the state of Micky's head.'

'I'm going to feed you my other fuckin' ear,' I heard Micky mumble.

I turned my head and looked straight into his eyes, noticing a newfound anger in them. Or maybe something else. And then my head started playing funny tricks on me and the sound of distant police sirens began. I looked around. Simon and David hadn't even registered. Maybe they had – or perhaps the sirens were just in my head. Wishful thinking. I turned to the rest of the cult members. Not one of them seemed to hear sirens either. I shook my head, sure that I was going insane.

Micky coughed, drawing my attention. 'I told you David was a soft bastard,' he said to me, winking.

I blinked at him, amazed that he could even speak. If someone had cut my ear off I would have died of shock. Unsure what to say, I nodded at him. His eyes moved downwards very quickly, pleading with me to follow them. I did. All I could see was the blood-soaked tissue and his ear. I looked up again.

'Soft, soft, soft,' he repeated. 'Ain't that right, David.'

I turned to David to see what he would do as my

mind invented more sirens which only I could hear. Or so it seemed. David was glaring at Micky, an intense hatred burning in his eyes.

'Shut up!' ordered Simon.

'Did yer brother make you do things, Davy?' asked Micky, his voice mocking. 'Were there tears and crying . . . *bullying*?'

I don't know how he did it, but Micky had touched a nerve. Cut it out with a blunt spoon. David turned his head away and let out a groaning sound from somewhere deep inside. Reaching into the pocket of his grey hooded top, he pulled out a hunting knife.

'Maybe you'd like me to cut off the other ear?' he spat at Micky.

I felt myself tense up as David made for Micky. That was when the imaginary sirens forced themselves into the real world. First one, then another, then another. The sound was muffled but it was definitely real and getting closer.

'Simon!' shouted the stocky woman from the foot of the steps, finally waking up. The shock of hearing anything from the other cult members made me jolt in my chair.

'Go!' Simon shouted back. 'Everyone out!'

'Where to?' asked one of the men, his eyes frantic.

'*Just go!*'

Pandemonium struck. As the cult members scrambled up the stairs, one after the other, Simon ran into the room where the computer was. David, maybe through shock, stood where he was, holding the knife.

Without warning he snapped, lunging at Micky. I watched, expecting Micky to scream as the knife tore into his flesh. But it didn't happen that way. Micky *did* cry out but it was a battle cry, and as David reached him, raging and off-balance, Micky's arms fell free and he moved sideways off the chair, using David's momentum against him. In a flash David was on his back, the knife in Micky's hand as he sat astride him.

'*Micky!*'

He turned to me and grinned and I could see that his teeth were covered in blood.

'Cut me free!'

He looked down at David, leaned back and brought his forehead crashing down while at the same time lifting David's head upwards. The sound of Micky's head smashing into David's nose was sickening, the bone splintering. David's head hit the ground with a thud.

'*Micky!* Simon's gonna get away!'

He reached across and used the knife to set me free. I sprang from my chair, noticing a spade that was sitting against the bunker wall. I grabbed it and walked quickly over to the room that Simon had entered. Just as I got there the door opened and Simon sprang out, a canvas laptop bag across his chest and a small silver gun in his left hand. Before he could blink I smashed him across the side of his head with the spade. He crashed sideways, away from the door, dropping the gun. The second swing of the spade knocked him to the floor.

I picked up the gun and turned to Micky, instantly

wishing that I hadn't. He was leaning over David, using the serrated knife to remove his left ear, sawing at it. Blood poured from the side of David's head, beginning to pool beneath it.

'*Micky* – leave him alone!' I cried out.

Instantly he seemed to snap out of some kind of daze. He looked up at me and then down at the mess he had made of David.

'Ah, Jesus!' he cried out, throwing the knife to one side and standing up.

'Come on! We've got to get Simon out of here and away from the police!'

Micky looked at me blankly so I explained what I meant.

'He'll never tell us what happened to Sophie if the police get him.'

Who knew what kind of story he'd make up? And, besides, by the time the police had cleared up the mess at the farmhouse and interviewed everyone . . .

'We have to get him out!' I repeated.

This time Micky really woke up. He nodded and in one movement, despite his injuries, he heaved Simon off the floor and threw him across his shoulder.

'Follow me,' he said, wincing in pain.

We made our way back to the car in pouring rain, across a sodden field, as quickly as we could. I knew that the right thing to do was head in the opposite direction, towards the flashing lights that were now surrounding the farmhouse. But we still didn't know where Sophie was and I didn't think we had time to wait for the police to handle it. We had Simon and, no matter what it took, I was going to make him tell me who had Sophie and exactly where she was.

When we got out into the lane the car was still there. Micky opened one of the rear doors and shoved Simon in before turning to me.

'Where's Anna?' he asked, holding the side of his head as though he'd only just realized that he had an ear missing. His legs seemed to wobble beneath him and he went down on one knee. 'Jesus . . . Jesus . . .' he repeated.

I went over and knelt down next to him. 'We have to get you to a hospital,' I told him.

He looked at me and tried to grin. 'Later,' he replied. 'It's not like they can put my bastard ear back on anyway . . .'

I put my hand in my pocket and pulled out a bloody piece of paper. In all the confusion I had picked up his ear. Micky looked at it, looked back at me and then roared with laughter.

'Come on!' he said when his laughter had subsided. 'I know a place . . .'

I shook my head. 'Let me go and find Anna first. The police are all over the place. Just sit tight here . . .'

Behind us we heard wood cracking. I spun round and up at the same time, alert and ready. But I couldn't see anyone. I studied the tree line for signs of someone or something but there was nothing.

'Stay here,' I told Micky. 'Keep an eye on Simon . . .
If he moves knock him out again.'

I walked slowly towards the trees, taking the gun out
of my front pocket and holding it in front of me. It's not
like I knew what I was doing. I'd never even *seen* a real
gun before, never mind fired one, but my brain was
telling me that it had to be pretty easy. I fingered the
trigger as I went on. It was pitch black.

Another rustling sound to my left made me take aim
but again I saw nothing in the darkness. I looked to my
right. Another noise.

The thing that I could hear scrambled away and I
dived in its direction, hoping that I wouldn't discharge
the gun accidentally and kill myself. I crashed through
soaking wet branches and dense thicket and caught
hold of a foot. The owner of the foot tried to work it
free from my grasp, kicking and twisting and turning,
but I held on tight and pulled myself alongside whoever it was. The person was on their front and I
grabbed at a shoulder as lightning crackled and an
instant clap of thunder shook the ground. I turned the
person over to see who it was. As another sheet of lightning fizzled and popped in the sky I made out her face.

'Get off me, you knob!' shouted Anna, the look of
relief in her eyes quickly making way for tears.

Thirty-one

Micky leaned through the space between the two front seats.

'Have either of you got any painkillers?' he asked.

'I haven't,' I told him.

'I have,' replied Anna. 'They're in my bag.'

She reached down and pulled out a pack of Ibuprofen tablets, handing them to Micky.

'Is there a CD cover in the glove box?' he continued.

Anna nodded, opened the glove box and gave him the cover of Faithless's greatest hits.

Micky smiled. 'God definitely is a DJ,' he told me, grinning like a madman.

I watched as he settled back into his seat, pushing Simon to one side. Simon stirred slightly but didn't wake up.

'You must have given him a good smack with that shovel,' Micky said.

He pulled a credit card out of his wallet before taking four pills from the blister pack. Placing them on the CD cover, he pressed down with the palm of his hand. I heard them crack under the weight. As I turned sharply into a blind corner, the headlights still off to avoid attention, I heard a grating sound. When I next looked in the rear-view mirror, Micky was grinding the powder up, using the credit card like someone would with cocaine. Then he rolled up a note and snorted the powder through his nostrils, one at a time, until most of it was gone.

'*Arrrghh!*'

Anna jumped in her seat and turned round. 'What the fuck are you doin'?' she asked, before realizing what was going on. 'Oh.'

Micky sat back and closed his eyes as I wondered again what kind of strength it took to have an ear cut off and still be able to speak or do anything. He must have been in agony.

'Fastest way into the bloodstream without an injection,' he mumbled, reading my mind.

'Where are we going?' I asked. 'I gotta put the head-lights on soon or we're gonna crash.'

'South,' he told me. 'Just keep heading south . . .'

I turned on the Faithless CD. It came on midway through a tune called 'Fatty Boo'. I hit the back button to start it again and turned the volume down.

'Where are we going?' I asked again, looking in my rear-view mirror to check that Simon was still unconscious.

'Head for Edinburgh,' he told me. 'And lend me your phone.'

I yawned deeply, threw Anna's phone back to Micky and asked Anna if she had anything in her bag that would keep me awake. She looked at me and shook her head.

'What the *hell* are we doing?' she asked.

Outside the horizon seemed to be getting lighter, only it couldn't have been. It was still only five in the morning. A trick of the light maybe, something I'd heard being described as the false dawn. Or just my tired and wired brain playing tricks on me. Sophie's face came to mind and then our song. I felt myself growing angrier by the second. Angry that we hadn't found Sophie and angry that Shining Moon hadn't told us where she was. I fought back an urge to try to wake him and make him tell me, and drove on.

I looked at Anna. 'Waiting till Simon comes round and then asking him some questions . . .'

In the end my anger couldn't wait. I tried and tried to hold it down, but all in vain. It built into a shard of pressure, right behind my eyes, stabbing and clawing at me. At around six a.m. I slammed on the brakes, bringing the car to a shuddering halt by the side of the dark, empty road. I leaped out and ran round to open Simon's door. He looked up at me and I punched him in the face twice and then dragged him by his hair out onto the verge, kicking at him until tears streamed from my eyes and Micky held me back. As Simon sat up, crying and sobbing like a baby, I spat at him.

'You tell me where she is right now or I swear I'll get my gun out and shoot you in your fucking eyes!' I told him.

'P-p-please!' begged Simon, cowering away from me as another car sped past us, not slowing for an instant. He watched it flash past, despair in his eyes.

'No one to help you now!' I told him. 'Where is she?'

Anna pulled me away and tried to calm me down. 'Not here!' she insisted, her face betraying the shock that she felt at my actions.

'*Here!*' I snapped back. 'He knows where she is.'

I turned back to Simon, who was still sobbing. 'Tell me right now or I'm gonna get that gun,' I warned.

He looked from me to Micky, searching our eyes for a shred of sympathy. But there was none to be had.

'OK,' he whimpered, 'but in the car, OK? It's cold out here.'

Micky sneered at him and then dragged him back to the car. 'Big man, eh?' he asked.

In the car Simon told us his story as he wiped blood onto his sleeve. I kept my eyes on him, not looking away once.

'Why Sophie?' I asked him.

'Why?' he repeated. 'Because she represents the pure – the pure innocence of Albion. She—'

I cut him off. 'Look, I've had enough of your new-age, racist shit. Just tell us what happened.'

Simon nodded and went on. 'We recruit wherever we can – festivals are just one area. You meet a lot of lost souls – young people who don't understand why they are so unhappy and disenchanted. We show them the light—'

'By brainwashing them with prejudice?' asked Anna. 'Nice . . .'

'It's my life – my purpose for being. Were *you* born for a purpose other than to be a consumer – a leech?' Simon asked me.

I nodded. 'Yeah – to *kill* you if you don't tell me what the fuck's goin' on. Who's the older man – the drag queen you were with – and where is my friend?'

'What older man?' he asked, although his eyes had flinched at the mention.

'You *know* which man. He was dressed as a woman and gave you a load of money at the festival. Someone saw you with him.'

Simon shrugged. 'I spoke to so many lost souls,' he replied, taking the piss.

'I'm gonna count to three,' I told him, rage burning in my eyes.

I pulled the gun from my pocket and pointed it at his face. 'One . . . two . . . thr—' I began.

'OK, OK!' he squealed. 'I'll tell you . . .'

I didn't move.

'He was . . . he . . .' spluttered Simon, before beginning to sob again.

'Right – that's it!' I shouted. 'Didn't they teach you any torture techniques in the forces?' I asked Micky.

He looked at me, his pupils like pinholes, wired. Fried by the painkillers he had snorted. 'Aye,' he said, grinning.

'Jit!' said Anna, looking concerned.

I turned to her and winked. She gave me a dirty look and looked away, out of the window.

266

'OK,' I said, turning back to Simon. 'I'm gonna give you some thinking time.'

'Huh?' he replied, but I ignored him.

'How long till we get to your place?' I asked Micky.

'Fifteen minutes – no more,' he told me. 'Why?'

I looked at Simon. 'That's what you've got,' I told him. 'That's all the time that stands between you and judgement day. Either you tell me where Sophie is by the time we get there or you die. And I'm not joking.'

I thought about what I'd just said and hoped that Simon believed me. That he wouldn't think it was just a bluff. After all, if I killed him, how were we gonna find Sophie? But from the sheer terror in his face I could tell that he did believe me. And then I began to wonder whether I *could* kill him if it came down to it. When it came, I didn't like the answer. I pulled the car out onto the road and gunned the accelerator.

Thirty-two

'Tell me.'

Simon lowered his head and his voice broke. 'We sell him girls,' he said, looking up at me with tears flowing down his cheeks.

I shook my head, thankful that Anna was asleep on Micky's sofa and that Micky was in the bedroom with a doctor friend he'd called on the way down.

'You *what?*' I asked.

'Girls – he . . . we sell him . . .' he added, before looking away.

'Why?' I asked, trying hard to get my head around what he was saying. But it was something no normal human being could understand. I felt cold inside.

'I . . . don't . . .' he spluttered.

'*Why?*' I demanded.

More tears began to fall down his face. 'We recruit so many runaways – people who choose to go missing. We give them a home and a family and— it all costs money. We're setting up a selective breeding programme and we need shelters and land and . . .'

'You *sell* them on to people like *him* – sick bastards who prey on young girls?'

'I didn't *know* he was—' he began.

'*You didn't know?* It never bothered you that he wanted to *buy* a girl . . . : ? Are you fucking *mad*?'

'I'm sorry,' he replied.

'*Sorry* – what the hell do I care if you're sorry?' I spat.

'She was one of them,' he continued. 'He took an instant liking to her – at the festival – seemed almost shy about it. He only saw her from distance – as though he was hiding from her. But he was adamant that he wanted her. I wasn't even sure that she would come with us. She was with some Australian man—'

'Ritter,' I told him.

He shrugged. 'Normally he visits us and takes his pick but this time it was different. He was obsessed with her from the moment he saw her . . .'

'Did he go with you to the festival?' I asked.

Simon shook his head. 'He just turned up.'

I looked at him over the top of the gun. The chill in my heart, the shock at what he was telling me, stopped me from firing.

'What next?' I asked.

'That depends on you – I'll tell the police every-thing,' he replied, almost begging. But he hadn't understood my meaning.

'What happened next with Sophie?' I said, making myself clearer.

'She walked over to where some of the brothers and sisters were waiting and started talking to them. The Australian guy left her there. I think he walked past us and went to get a drink from a beer tent.'

'Did he see the man you were with?'

Simon nodded. 'He said something to him as he passed – something about his dress being the wrong colour.'

'What's his name?' I asked.

'You just told me – Ritter, wasn't it?'

'The *drag* queen,' I spat out. 'Don't start taking the piss again.'

Simon shook his head. 'I don't *know* his name,' he told me. 'He just joined our message boards on MSN . . .'

I nodded but inside I had a hunch that Simon was lying about the man's name. He knew it but maybe he was too scared to tell me. I changed tack, sensing something. 'What was his screen name?' I asked hurriedly.

'The Angel Collector.'

My brain went haywire. The man that I'd first heard about in Tooting. The man who had taken Claire Burrows. The same man who had taken Sophie. Then Sophie's face filled my mind's eye. I wanted to ask Simon more, now there was no doubt that he was the older man Corey had told me about – the tranny – but I decided to bide my time.

'What happened next – with Sophie?' I asked instead.

Simon gulped down air and looked away. 'I know it was wrong,' he pleaded. 'But I didn't *know*. If I had known I—'

I shook my head and inched the gun forward.

'Don't even start,' I told him. 'I want to know exactly what happened. Any reaction I have to it – well, you're just gonna have to deal with it.'

'Oh Jesus,' he whimpered. 'I need the toilet . . .'

I shook my head. 'Tell me,' I demanded again.

He looked down into his lap, where a dark, wet patch was growing larger on his trousers. 'I asked David to take her to one side. He walked her over to one of our vans and spoke to her. I followed them and opened the van door, pretending to look for something and . . . Oh God, please don't hurt me . . . I . . . I . . .'

I leaned forward and pressed the barrel of the gun against the middle of his forehead. 'Tell me,' I whispered.

'David covered her mouth, picked her up and threw her into the van. Then he knocked her out—'

'*How?*'

'He . . . he . . . punched her!' Simon sobbed.

'How *much?*' I demanded.

'Huh?'

'For Sophie – how much did you get for sending her away with that man?'

'Two . . . two thousand pounds . . .'

Something in my head clicked so hard that I thought my veins might pop with the pressure. My sight went for a split second and then I was on Simon, holding him down by the throat, squeezing with one hand while the other shoved the barrel up against his nostrils. He tried to fight back but his hands were tied behind his back. Eventually he stopped and I let him go. He had turned a deep shade of red and coughed his guts up.

I stepped back and looked at him. 'Where is she?' I asked calmly, surprising myself. 'Is she alive?'

Simon coughed some more before replying. 'I don't know,' he told me. 'He told me that he doesn't harm them. Just keeps them for a bit – long enough to teach them the truth about Albion—'

'*Them* – how many have there been?'

He shrugged. 'Maybe ten – I don't know . . .'

'Was one of them called Claire Burrows?' I demanded.

'Yes!'

'Did you take her from the festival too?'

'No – I swear . . . she was earlier . . .'

His answer didn't compute. From what Stephen had told me, I knew that Claire Burrows had been seen at the festival. The police had told him as much. Somewhere in my brain a synaptic wave cracked and popped and fizzed. Then the wiring came loose and it began to dawn on me. A slow, creeping realization that began to tear down everything I thought I knew.

'And how many has he brought back?' I asked, snapping out of it.

Simon looked down at the floor and whispered something.

'Speak up!' I demanded.

'None,' he said in a low voice.

My stomach turned over. The only thing that stopped me from trying to murder Simon was the fact that I wanted to know more. 'None at all?'

Simon shrugged. 'We had a new one for him but he didn't take her. He said that he'd found a new sister to work on . . . somewhere closer . . .'

'I don't understand – what new one? Another girl?'

'Yes.' Simon nodded.

Suddenly Anna's mobile phone began to vibrate in my pocket. I pulled it out and looked at the number. It had a Birmingham code. Jamie.

'What's happened?' he asked me as soon as I answered. 'I've been calling and calling your phone. It's dead.'

'I can't explain right now,' I told him. 'Did Ritter get back to you?'

'I've got him on MSN right now,' replied Jamie, making my heart jump. In the back of my head that deep, dark dread was beginning to grow larger.

'Does he know something?'

'Yeah – he did see the bloke you were on about, mate – the tranny or whatever he is. He's on one of the photos you emailed. In the background. I rang straight away – couldn't get you. So I called Anna.'

I looked at Simon and tried to keep my composure. But inside I was on fire . . .

'You still there?' asked Jamie, sounding concerned.

'Yeah – *which* photo?'

'Huh?'

'*Which* photo does he mean?'

'Hang on, mate – I'll ask him . . .'

I lowered the phone from my ear and put it on speakerphone. Then I turned to Simon.

'Where's Sophie and what's the name of the man you sold her to? And this time don't lie to me or I will blow your brains out. Tell me his real name.' I spat out the words.

Simon looked at me. He paused for a moment, just long enough for Jamie to start speaking on the phone again.

'Jit . . . you there?'

'Yeah,' I replied.

Jamie told me which photo Ritter was on about at exactly the same time as Simon gave me the older man's name. Only I already knew what both were going to say. It had been there all along. I don't know how or why but it had been there. Not that knowing made the shock any easier to deal with.

'How can he be sure?' I asked Jamie frantically. 'In the picture he's looking at the man *isn't* in drag . . .'

'Hang on – I'll double check,' he replied.

It took him a few moments to get back to me. In that short amount of time I thought my head was going to explode. I felt sick.

'Ritter reckons he saw the bloke right up close – says he is absolutely sure it's the same fella . . . the one that was wearing women's clobber,' said Jamie.

My heart jumped. The name that Simon had given me matched the name of the person on the photo Ritter was looking at. A photo that I had sent from my *own* phone. A family and friends photo, taken at one of Sophie's birthday parties . . .

I dropped the phone, turned the gun round so that I was holding the barrel and started to smash it over Simon's head, over and over. I was raging, screaming until my lungs caught fire.

'*No! No! No!*'

And then I felt Micky and Anna pulling me away for the second time in an hour.

'What's happened?' asked Anna continually as I hid my face in my hands and cried.

I left twenty minutes later. Anna watched me go with confusion written all over her face.

'Just call the police and tell them to come here,' I told her, taking her phone out of my pocket and giving it to her. 'Then call Jamie and get him to tell you what he told me . . .'

'But I don't understand . . .' she said again.

'Just do it, Anna, please.'

Micky came out after me. 'I got Simon's phone off him,' he told me as he handed it to me. 'Although he didn't put up a fight – I think you've fractured his skull.'

I blinked in Edinburgh's early morning light as the traffic slowly began to build up with people setting out for work. It felt like I was walking through a waking nightmare. I felt numb from the inside out. My mind crawled with a million and one thoughts, none of which fitted together into anything I could keep hold of.

'I don't understand,' Micky said.

'Don't matter,' I told him. 'It's done now. I'm sorry about your ear.'

'So am I,' he said.

'You need to get to a hospital . . .'

He nodded. 'My friend put something on it in the bedroom – while you were talking to Simon.'

'You still need to go,' I repeated.

'After we call the police – although if Sophie's father is on his way . . .'

I shook my head. 'We haven't got time to wait for them,' I told him. 'I'll call him from the road – get the locals in. I've left a quick note on the table. Don't open it until they arrive – please . . .'

He nodded.

'And thanks,' I added. 'You saved my life and I don't even know who you are apart from your name.'

'Yes, you do,' he said to me. 'A friend . . .'

I walked over to my cousin's car, got in and set off. My journey, the final part of it, was about to take me south, back into England and right into the heart of a darkness that was already making my soul bleed.

Thirty-three

Stephen rang me while I was on the road. Not me exactly, but Simon, as it was his phone that I had. I looked down at it as I sat in traffic on the M1.

'I've been sending you text messages all night,' he told me, once he'd realized that it was me he was talking to. The shock, if he'd felt any, didn't register at all in his voice.

'Why?' I asked. 'Why did you do it?'

'From Jenna's phone,' he added, ignoring my question. 'Does that make you angry? I know how you can get angry. Sophie told me . . .'

I gulped down air about three times, trying to stop myself from being sick. It took me a minute or two to speak. He said nothing in the meantime, simply breathing normally down the phone.

'Is she alive?' I asked, dreading what his answer would be. 'I know you've killed Sophie but Jenna *better* be alive . . .'

'And why *is* that, Jit? Are you on your way to kill *me*?'

'Yeah,' I replied.

'But you don't even know where I am.'

I knew he was right but I also had a feeling that he wanted to see me. Something didn't sit right, even beyond the awful things that had happened. The awful truth that I had learned.

'Tell me,' I said. 'You know you want to . . .'

'Maybe I do. But then again, perhaps I'd like to tie up a few loose ends first. She looks lovely in the morning, just as she's about to wake up . . .'

My heart sank. 'Which one?' I asked. 'You've had so many . . .'

'Oh – you've been talking to Brother Simon. I knew he was all talk. Did you find their pathetic little cult funny? I know I did.'

'When did you take Jenna?' I asked, ignoring his question about Shining Moon.

'I can't quite remember . . .'

I thought for a moment. 'Why?' was all I could come up with.

'Oh come on, Jit – with your amazing IQ? Surely you can work it out?' he sneered. 'You saw the same things in her that you saw in *my* angel . . . you *know* you did.'

So many images flashed through my head. So many memories, so many late nights sitting with him and Sophie, listening to music and talking about all kinds of stuff. So many lies, so many lies . . .

'I'm going to cut out your heart,' I said quietly.

'I'm sorry?' he replied.

'You heard me . . . Where's Imogen? Did you kill her too?'

He began to chuckle softly. I let him continue until he was ready to stop.

'Oh, I'm forgetting,' I said when he was quiet. 'Imogen doesn't fit your pattern, does she?'

'Pattern?' he asked, sounding amused. 'You make me sound like a *serial* killer. What's next – telling me about my modus operandi? How very clichéd . . .'

'How many girls *have* you killed?'

'Liberated,' he said, like he was correcting me.

'How *many*?'

He paused for a while and I heard his breathing change from slow and deliberate to fast and wheezing.

'Maybe nine,' he told me. 'Maybe ten – could even be more. Or *less* . . .'

'Stephen—'

'*Don't!*' he shouted down the line, making me jump. I'd never heard him raise his voice so high.

'Fuck off,' I said, my default reply when I had nothing else to say.

He calmed down before saying more. 'Don't try and take me back,' he said.

'Back to *where*?' I asked, confused.

'To that life,' he continued. 'You can't pacify me by calling me Stephen. I'm not him – he was constructed – don't you see that? The only reason I even wanted a family was to create my own angel . . .'

I let Stephen talk on for a bit. In my head I wondered about what had made him the killer that he was and why no one seemed to have picked up on it. So many girls and he hadn't betrayed a thing. But then

I thought of all the pictures I'd ever seen of serial killers. Not one that I could recall had a memorable face. There was no sign on any of their foreheads, pointing to their complete lack of humanity. They always looked so ordinary.

'You're a very good actor,' I told him when he'd finished talking.

'There was never an act,' he claimed. 'I've always been two people. None of you ever worked it out. Now I've had to do that for you . . . *lead* you to me.'

'You see,' I began, 'that's the part I don't get. Why would you *help* me to find you? You gave me all that money and rang me all the time and . . .'

'Go on,' he sneered. 'It's ticking over now, isn't it — that brain of yours?'

'*Shit* . . .'

'I take it you've worked out that the texts that came after Sophie became mine — they all came from me?'

'The ones that were sent after she went missing? All those frantic pleas . . . ?'

'Exactly, Jit.'

I slowed the car down and pulled across two lanes onto the hard shoulder. Undoing my seat belt, I leaned across the passenger seat, watched the window whirring its way down and then puked out of the side of the car. I could hear Stephen laughing. When I was done I sat back in the driver's seat and put the phone back to my ear.

'Everything you did,' he boasted. 'Even part of your reason for wanting to find Sophie. Your whole reason for *being* – it was all orchestrated by me . . .'

'Why?' I croaked, my throat sore and dry.

'Because she loved *you*,' he told me. 'Not *me*, like she should have done. It was always about *you* from the moment she started at that *damn* school. And then you were always at the house and I had to sit there, *smiling* at you. Pretending to *like* you when all the time I wanted to cave your skull in with a rock and—' He caught himself getting angry and paused before calming down again.

'And she was *my* angel,' he told me. 'I *created* her. I *made* her. She was *mine* . . .'

I thought about what he was saying but *still* something didn't sit right. If it had been about Sophie and me – why all the others?

'You're not telling me something,' I said as coolly as I could manage.

'Why don't you come and see me?' Stephen suggested. 'Maybe I'll tell you . . .'

'You want this to end, don't you?' I asked.

'Yes, Jit,' he replied.

I asked him to tell me where he was. I had to promise him something in return.

'I'll come alone,' I said. 'No tricks, no funny business . . . but I have to know where Sophie is. I promised I'd find her and even if you have killed her – I need to know where she is, OK?'

'We'll see,' he replied.

'*No!*' I shouted. 'That's the deal . . . or I call the police right now.'

'OK,' he said, relenting.

'One more thing, Stephen.'

'What's that, Jit?'

'Let Jenna go . . .'

'No,' he said, very calmly. 'My collection is not complete—'

'Stephen . . .'

'OK,' he replied. 'Let's play just *one* more game. I'll give you a chance. If you can get to me before midday then perhaps you can stop me. Any later and she joins the others – agreed?'

I nodded, knowing that I didn't really have any choice.

'And if I even so much as *sense* a police presence, she dies . . .' he added menacingly.

'Agreed.'

Then he told me where he was . . .

I snapped the phone shut and threw it into the foot well on the passenger side. Then I pulled back out into the traffic and drove like a lunatic back to Leicester, to confront a real-life demon.

Jenna watched Stephen walk into the room and approach the bed that Sophie was tied to. He began to untie her, leaving her gag in place. Sophie's eyes were frantic, searching the room in despair. When she made eye contact Jenna looked away for a second. But then she looked back. There were tears flowing freely down Sophie's cheeks.

Jenna wondered whether she should try and loosen her own ties, which didn't feel as tight as they had. She began to flex her wrists, which were tied behind her, and, sure enough, there was movement.

As Stephen lifted an emaciated Sophie onto his shoulders Jenna realized that one of her hands was almost free. Stephen had seemed preoccupied when he'd tied her up an hour earlier. There had been none of his swagger or cruelty. At least not extreme cruelty. And he'd made a mistake.

'You wait there, angel,' he said to Jenna. 'I'll just get Sophie ready and then it'll be your turn. We're expecting guests so we've got to look our best, haven't we?'

Jenna stopped moving her hands and stayed as still as she could. What did he mean by 'guests'? Her heart started to pound faster and faster. Whoever it was, it couldn't be a good thing or he would have panicked. She watched him leave the room, an exact replica of Sophie's real bedroom, she realized now, built into a warehouse of some sort, and when he'd gone she began to loosen her hands with increased urgency. She had to get free.

When Stephen returned fifteen minutes or so later Jenna was waiting for him, or so she thought. He was wearing a floral-print dress, with seamed stockings and black high heels. On his head was a curly blonde wig and his lips were covered in bright red lipstick, which looked as though a blind child had applied it. Jenna froze as he walked into range and the piece of metal pipe she'd been holding, ready to crack open his skull with, fell to the floor with a clunking sound. He looked at her and shook his head slowly.

'Now that's not very nice,' he told her. 'Especially as your lovely friend Jit is on his way here to rescue you . . .'

'What?' she asked, her mouth open and her heart pounding even harder, if that was possible.

'But I'm afraid he's only expecting one of you to be alive and I don't want to disappoint him. It's just a shame that you seem to have made my decision for me. One of you is going to pay for being such a naughty angel. Can you guess who it will be?'

Jenna made to move but Stephen caught her and held her tightly. Then he slapped her about the face several times. When he was sure that she wouldn't try to run again he dragged her out of the recreated bedroom, chuckling to himself.

'Such naughty angels . . .'

Thirty-four

It had started to snow by the time I reached the door, completely the wrong weather for April. But the perfect weather to mirror how disjointed I felt. It was all wrong. Deeply, badly wrong. At least I was calmer now – the horror I felt had been put on a back burner, taking its place in a queue of emotions that I was going to have to deal with sooner or later. For now there was only Stephen and how I was going to stop him. Nothing else mattered.

The building in front of me looked like a long abandoned warehouse – one that smelled as though it had been used for agricultural purposes. Next to it, about fifty metres down a muddy track, was a stone cottage that had also seen better days, and beside that was Stephen's car. I had parked a lot further back, out by the little private road that I'd been directed to. The busy A6 was barely a mile away but it might as well have been in a different country. The old farm was well hidden, away from prying eyes, which made sense. If you were a killer with bodies to hide.

The door was hanging open, a rusty padlock sitting on the ground in front of it. A light was on inside and

I could hear faint music although I couldn't work out what it was. I edged inside slowly, careful to watch my every step and looking around like a cop on a TV show. When I was satisfied that I wasn't about to get jumped I decided to move a little faster, determined to reach Stephen before he could do anything to Jenna.

The light source was about ten metres away, towards the centre of the vast space, which had been divided up with partitions. I walked towards the source, looking for a weapon of some sort. Not that I didn't already have a weapon – I wasn't stupid. I had the gun that I'd taken from Simon – but that was my edge. My surprise. And I didn't want to reveal my hand too soon.

When I reached the partitioned room from which the light was coming I noticed that it too had a padlocked door. The door was hanging open, just as the one outside had been. I felt myself tense up as someone turned up the music. It was Sophie's song. Unsure of whether I was doing the right thing or not, I stepped into the room and saw Sophie and Jenna tied to chairs, gagged and half naked, and Stephen, dressed in drag, standing behind them.

My head exploded with emotions as I stared into Sophie's blue eyes for the first time in so long. I felt as if my heart might pop and I stood where I was, like a dickhead, unable to move. She was alive! Tears began to work their way down my cheeks. Even if I had wanted to keep them back, I couldn't have. I stood paralysed, as emotion after emotion and wave after wave of memory flooded through my head. Sophie . . .

Stephen saw my paralysis too and he played on it.

'Hello, Jit,' he said, smiling. 'Like the song? I know it was one of your favourites . . . seems to encapsulate the mood, doesn't it?'

He looked grotesque. Like someone had asked him to come up with the worst cross-dressing look ever. I tried to speak but words failed me. I knew that he was a cross-dresser but I hadn't been ready for what I could see standing before me. The normal, everyday father turned killer. I struggled to keep my eyes from his face.

'You *see*?' he sneered. 'You were wrong. I've kept her alive for you . . . for so long. She's my special angel, the centrepiece of my collection. Not like the others. They were just practice. This is my finale . . .'

I tore my gaze away from Stephen to check on Jenna. I looked at her bruised and swollen face, her scared eyes. Then I looked back at Sophie, whose eyes seemed to plead with me. She looked so thin, so frail. Her hair was ragged and her bones stuck out, as though they might soon pierce the skin. The gun, nestling against the small of my back, felt cold and sharp and ready. I felt its grip begin to take over but I held it off. I had to know.

'Why?' I asked Stephen.

'*Why? Why?*' he mimicked in a high-pitched voice. 'Because this is what I was made to be . . .' He looked down at his clothes and then at me. He was grinning.

'She wanted a girl – an angel,' he told me. 'But I was a boy and boys can't be angels. They're too rude and dirty and they don't look good in pretty dresses . . .'

'Who?' I asked.

'Mother,' he replied.

I felt the urge to smirk but I held it in check. Stephen was a freak and I told him so.

'What do you know?' he asked me, getting angry.

I shook my head, keeping my eyes firmly on the girls.

'The only time she ever showed me any love, any warmth . . . no angel, no love . . .' he continued, his voice beginning to break.

'But what does that have to do with Sophie and Jenna?' I asked, hoping that he would try and explain things. I needed him to explain things.

'Everything,' he replied.

'What does that mean?' I asked, glancing at Sophie before looking back into his eyes.

'Nothing to you . . . but then you will never understand. I made Sophie . . . created her. Do you think I actually wanted to have a family? It was all a means to an end. I even chose her mother because she had blonde hair—'

'But that's crazy,' I heard myself say, realizing how ridiculous it sounded. 'You could never have been certain she would look the way you needed her to look. What if she'd had brown hair, brown eyes?'

'Then she would have been safe, wouldn't she?' he sneered at me.

'I still don't get it,' I added. 'You had her whole life to do what you've done – why wait until the festival?'

'Ah . . . I wondered whether you would ask me that.

The answer, Jit, should be more than obvious. Angels are innocent – it is in their nature. They are pure and clean. She was about to leave me. Go out into the big wide world where she would have met more men like you, losing the one thing that made her so special . . .'

'You?' I asked.

'No,' he replied softly. 'Innocence . . . And once it's gone it never returns – I had to stop that from happening . . .'

'But why choose a place with so many potential witnesses?'

'I'm far too good to let a few thousand people bother me,' he boasted. 'And, besides, I had Simon and his friends to do my dirty work for me . . .'

'But you were seen,' I reminded him.

'Yes, I was, but it still took my own actions to guide you to me, didn't it? Had I wanted to stay anonymous I would have . . . it was all down to me.'

'And Jenna?' I asked.

'Another angel,' he explained. 'One that I'd watched for so long . . . It seemed a shame not to add her to it.'

'To what,' I asked, looking at Jenna.

'To my collection . . .' he replied.

'How many others?' I asked again, hoping that he would tell me. He didn't.

'What does that matter now?' he said. 'This is the endgame. The rest of it was practice – honing myself in readiness for the final act. You've been played like the obsessive fool that you are and now I've got you exactly where I want you. When the police arrive, you will be left – the last man standing, ready to explain my life's work . . .'

'Where will you be?'

Stephen shifted from foot to foot and then looked away, towards his daughter. 'I'll be with my angels, for ever,' he told me.

'Only one problem with that,' I told him. 'I haven't called the police.'

He looked at me and shook his head. 'No – you followed your instructions right to the last. I called them.'

'Why? That doesn't make any sense . . .' I said.

'Not to you . . .' he replied as I looked back at Jenna.

Jenna's eyes widened, as if she was trying to warn me about something. I looked around and saw nothing except for a chest freezer in the corner of the room, also padlocked. The floor was covered in threadbare sea-grass matting, in places completely worn away. In the spots where I could see the concrete floor there were dark patches and what looked like congealed matter. I moved slightly further into the room and had a closer look. That was when I realized that I was standing in the place where he killed them. There was a cloying, metallic smell, as well as the deeply ingrained odour of human waste. It was a human abattoir. I almost doubled over in disgust and pain and rage.

'You know all those text messages . . . ?' Stephen said as the song looped over and began again. 'The ones that you got after I'd taken Sophie? Even the one from Claire came from me . . .'

I thought about Claire's message, telling me to leave Sophie alone – she never wanted to see me again. I felt myself blinking with rage but I held it back.

'What about the last one?' I asked him, feeling tears welling in my eyes. 'The one about her loving me and wanting me back . . . ?'

He smiled. 'That was one of the things she said to me,' he explained, 'when I mentioned your name . . . She was in love with you.'

I gulped down air and looked over at Sophie, who had tears streaming down her emaciated face. My emotions twisted and turned like shoals of fish trying to escape a predator.

'So what?' I asked, even though razor-sharp knives stabbed at my guts.

'I controlled everything you did, Jit. Every night you spent lying awake, wishing you still had her. Every piece of rage and sadness. Every thought of finding her – it was all me . . .'

I struggled to find something to say. Struggled to keep my temper in check. Struggled to hold myself back. Looking back now, I wish in some ways that I hadn't.

Stephen sensed that I was lost. He leaned down behind Jenna and started to do something. I thought about pulling the gun but still something stopped me. Suddenly Jenna was ungagged and Stephen had her in his grasp, his forearm locked tightly round her throat from behind, a long-bladed knife swinging in his free hand.

'Don't move an inch,' he warned, 'or I'll cut her head off before you can blink.'

He dragged her towards the chest freezer. As he approached it I noticed that its padlock had a key in it. He tapped the key with the blade.

'Open it!' he told her.

Jenna wriggled a little but did as she was told, turning the key and loosening the lock. Then he tapped the top of the freezer with the knife.

'Lift the lid,' he demanded.

Jenna froze for a moment. He tightened his grip and swore at her.

'Do it!'

She did as he asked and the lid came up. I stood and watched as Jenna seemed to recoil in horror. Stephen brought his knife hand across her throat and used his free hand to reach into the freezer and lift something out. He turned to me with a plastic bag in his hand and threw it across the floor. It bounced twice before splitting open. A severed head fell out.

'Say hello to Claire,' said Stephen, grinning like the madman he was. Then he pulled out another. 'And this one . . . this is Kylie Simmons . . .'

Another severed head rolled towards my feet.

Yet again I had to force back the bile that was burning its way up my gullet and into my throat. I gagged twice and spat out the vile fluid. My eyes began to water. I glared at Stephen.

'All this because you had to wear a dress?' I replied.

'And now,' he sneered menacingly, 'it's time for the final act . . .'

I didn't have time to blink. No time to move. In my mind he drew the blade silently and quickly across Jenna's throat. A bloody smile gaped open across her pale skin. Blood gushed like a torrent down onto her bare chest. Her eyes widened in shock and then the realization that she was experiencing her last few seconds on earth took hold. Terror followed the shock. And then, as he let her go, she slid to the floor.

But it didn't happen that way. Instead I heard him cry out as Jenna stamped on his foot and then turned and wriggled free. He looked straight at me and roared in anger. His face changed completely, twisted in rage. Without warning he charged towards me, the knife held high above his head. I pulled out the gun, pointed it and fired. The first shot missed. The second caught him below the left collarbone. The third, fourth and fifth shots peppered his chest, little crimson flowers exploding into full bloom. He staggered back, his momentum halted, standing for a second, his eyes never leaving mine, before he screamed and then crashed backwards. His skull cracked sickeningly against the concrete floor and he groaned for a few moments before blood bubbled up through his mouth like cherry soda foam. Then he was still.

I stood and looked at Stephen's body for a moment or two before dropping the gun to the floor and making my way over to Jenna who, with trembling hands, was trying to untie Sophie. Even when Sophie's gag was removed and she stood shaking un-controllably, neither of them said anything.

'Let's get outside,' I said gently, helping them to their feet and removing my jacket and top for them to put on.

Once they were covered up I put my arm round Sophie and, with Jenna, walked her out into the snow and the grey afternoon light. I stood for a moment and looked at her. Then I kissed her on the forehead.

'I'm sorry,' I told her, fighting back a tidal wave of emotions.

Sophie looked at me and shook her head but still she said nothing. Unsure of what to do or what else to say, I put my arms round her and pulled her towards me. Behind me, back in the old warehouse, Sophie's song played on . . .

RANI & SUKH
Bali Rai

'Man, she's wicked like one of them Bollywood
actresses . . .'

Sukh reckons Rani is the most fanciable girl in school.
She's got just the kind of look he goes for . . .

Rani can't stop thinking about Sukh either.
Talk about fit. Beautiful amber-brown eyes,
like pools you could jump into . . .

But Rani is a Sandhu, and Sukh is a Bains – and
sometimes names can lead to terrible trouble . . .

A powerful and gripping novel that sweeps the reader
from modern-day Britain to the Punjab in the 1960s and
back again in a ceaseless cycle of tragedy and conflict.

CORGI BOOKS

978 0 552 54890 8

THE LAST TABOO
Bali Rai

*'Tyrone leaned across the table and gave me a long kiss.
When I eventually opened my eyes I saw an Asian couple,
middle-aged, on the next table along. You know that
phrase – if looks could kill? Well, I was dead.'*

Simran falls for Tyrone the moment she spots him in the crowd.
He's gorgeous. Even better, he fancies her back.
But there's one big problem: Tyrone is black.

It's the last taboo for an Asian girl – and one that others
will do anything to enforce . . .

Also by the multi award-winning author Bali Rai:

(un)arranged marriage – 'Absorbing' *Observer*

The Crew – 'A jewel of a book' *Independent*

Rani & Sukh – 'Overwhelmingly powerful' *The Bookseller*

The Whisper – 'Energy and verbal brilliance
evident on every page' *TES*

A hard-hitting novel about two teenagers facing up to the
consequences of racial prejudice between asian and black
communities, from award-winning author Bali Rai.

978 0 552 55301 8